WHERE EVIL LIVES

Where Evil Lives

A.F. WINTER

As with the first book in this trilogy, I would like to dedicate this book on love, to my parents, S & M, who found each other over seventy years ago, and have kept it going through good and bad times, for richer and poorer, in sickness and in health.

Prologue (Sort of)

In a book, the introductory sections before the main text are called "front matter." This includes elements like a preface, foreword, introduction, and prologue.

None of these seems quite right for what I am trying to communicate to the reader.

A preface is written by the author and explains their background and motivation for writing the book. This is not why I am writing this beginning bit, but as long as we are here...

I have written Cinderella's End Part Two because I have already written Part One. I decided very soon after that previous writing that this needed to be a trilogy and not because it was a commercial success. The real reason was that I read W.B. Yeats' The Island of Statues shortly after finishing Part One. I knew then that it would have three parts, and the final part would end in a place similar to Yeats' Island. I had no idea what would happen in part two. So, I cannot say that this is a preface.

A foreword is written by someone other than the author and introduces the book to the reader. Obviously, this is written by the author, although, if I had my druthers, and I seem to have misplaced my druthers for the moment, I would have liked to have Mr. Yeats write the foreword, in which he would not only introduce the reader to Part Two but forgive the writer for stealing his island idea albeit 85 years after his death. Pity. Pity all around.

An introduction delves into the main topics and prepares the reader for the material that follows. Prepare the reader? OK, guys, hold on to your seats! Do you feel prepared? I must confess that this is a vastly different type of book from its predecessor. Cinderella's End Part One, and I did not put part one on it because, at the time of its writing, there wasn't going to be a part two. The first part is more of an emotional roller coaster with poor Cinderella trying to figure out her place in the royal family. The second part, which you will soon find out if you ever get past this section, is a Gothic romance horror story. I hope you feel better prepared.

A prologue, common in fiction, sets the stage for the story. Part Two begins almost immediately after Part One concludes. I fear this is not a prologue either because I have not yet shared the important bits.

So, this explanation is not any of those things, but it should be at the beginning of this novel, so I will call it a preintrologue, just because it seems like it would be difficult to say, and I enjoy making up new words. I was going to use protologue, which sounds very cool, but it was already taken by the scientific community and has nothing to do with literature.

Three things I would like to make clear with my preintrologue.

One. I have included a summary of Cinderella's End Part One at the end of the book, or in the postextrologue. I have included this, so if you didn't read the first part, you can quickly get up to speed. If you have read the first part, this could serve as a refresher.

Two. I have included a glossary of all the places and people mentioned in the first two books, following the postextrologue. This will be immensely helpful because, at times, this trilogy reads more like a Chekhov play than a Gothic romance or horror story.

Three. And this part is most interesting to me, is how I use Cinderella and Princess Ella. Both names refer to the same person, the poor waif whom Prince John married and brought to the castle to live happily ever after. I generally use Cinderella when I want the reader to understand the inner turmoil of the leading character and her lack of self-worth. Princess Ella is used as the character grows more confident in her self-worth. Other characters also used these names in different ways. Cinderella could be used as an idea that if you are good and keep your mouth shut, you will be rescued and live happily. In this instance, she is a symbol of hope. Others use Cinderella to put her in her place, that she does not deserve to live in a fancy castle and wear pretty dresses. Here, her name is used to remind her that her social standing could be transitory, and she will always be a servant at her core.

To a lesser degree, I do the same thing with Abby, Princess Anne's servant. I use Abigail when I want the reader to see her as a person, and Abby when she is to be viewed as a thing, and most people in the castle view her in less than human terms. Sometimes, Prince John and Princess Ella call her Abby, but they are using it as a term of endearment because they genuinely care for this serving girl brought to their home.

Both characters have inner struggles. Both have secrets.

So, I use their names interchangeably for a purpose. You may try to figure out why I made each choice, or you could just accept that Cinderella is Princess Ella and Abby, at times, is Abigail.

I hope you enjoy reading Cinderella's End Part Two and, when it comes out, Part Three.

A.F. Winter
May 2025

$$\sim 1 \sim$$

"Hello," was the first word softly spoken by Prince John to his wife after the long day of greeting well-wishers on his return.

The royal court finally left. The queen and Prince George retired, and Princess Anne had been shown to her room. Prince John spent a few minutes talking to his father before returning to his apartment. Cinderella and John were alone, as husband and wife, for the first time in many years, and all he could think of to say was hello.

"Hello," Cinderella answered.

He looked older, but he also looked kinder.

"I am sorry it took me so long to bring Anne home. I should never have left you for all these years."

She looked older and frailer than the last time he saw her. Her body shook slightly.

They were different. They had changed in John's absence. They were strangers.

This moment, anticipated for so long, passed in awkwardness. And now the moment was gone.

They were still distant. They were still strangers. Now, the distance had faded, but their emotional gap seemed vast.

They were no longer the young man and woman falling in love at the ball. But who were they? And could they be those young, hopeful lovers again? If true love could sprout in the desert, then couldn't hard work and understanding revive even the most wilted feelings?

He instinctively moved toward her, and she allowed his embrace. His touch felt unnatural, as if they didn't belong together. They remained frozen in that interminable unnaturalness for several moments until they could no longer bear it. Finally, she took a small step back, and he released her.

"I am sorry, too. Today has been exhausting. I am happy that you have returned, my liege. I am sure I will be better in the morning."

"Very well, Ella, but I am not your ruler; you are my equal. I owe you my life. Whenever I thought of giving up, I thought of you and had the strength to continue. You think I am a stranger to you. I am a stranger to myself. I promise you, Ella, whatever we need to do, I will do it to the last measure of my strength. Please give me the chance."

Cinderella managed an insecure smile to please the prince. She did not know whether his promises were true, but he seemed to believe his words.

"Yes, my lord," she said as she turned to prepare for bed.

He watched her close the door to their bedroom.

~ 2 ~

Spontaneous celebrations erupted throughout the city when the news trickled down to the people that Prince John had returned and rescued the princess. In every square and every back street of Aristal, people rejoiced, greeting their neighbors whom they hadn't spoken to in years, forgiving debt, and giving charity to the poor. Everyone felt a dark cloud had been lifted from the kingdom. Traveling players performed the story in a play quickly written entitled *Anne Abducted.*

"Welcome, ladies and gentlemen," the lead actor strutted to the center of the stage hastily constructed in the town's main square. "But beware and protect your children! Because evil has come to our city."

Just then, a witch appeared in a puff of smoke and rushed to the center of the stage, scaring both child and parent alike.

"This is the evil witch, Pesta," the player continued. "Who took the innocent Princess Anne out of her bed one night and brought the child to her terrible castle in the dark forest."

Children cried, and the adults in the audience gasped at the real-life horror story unfolding before their eyes.

"But have no fear. The great Prince John rescued the helpless princess."

A handsome actor appeared and waved to the crowd, who cheered the noble prince.

"And brought her back to the palace, uniting the royal family so all is right in our kingdom."

The actors who played Anne and Cinderella ran onstage, and all three hugged each other.

"And the nobility and, hence, the people of Bain will live happily ever after. Please kindly hear our humble performance, and if it is pleasing to you, a coin or two in our hat would allow us to play our play another day!"

With a flourish of his hand, the player left the stage, and the action began.

~ 3 ~

Cinderella looked out the castle window at the celebrations in the streets below. She was relieved to have her husband and daughter back. *At last,* she thought, *we shall have peace and happiness.* Neither actually existed, but everyone tried their best.

She joined her family at the dining table, where a feast was taking place. The guests were laughing, singing, and toasting their good fortune. Cinderella looked around at the joyful participants. She slowly sipped the wine in her goblet, holding on to its taste in order not to be swept away by the turmoil around her. She needed to hold on to her hope that things might end happily. Too much drink and her fears would slip out.

Prince John sat beside her. Feeling her worry, he took her hand, raised it to his lips, and kissed it. She smiled at him.

"Don't worry, my darling," he whispered in her ear. "Soon, all these people will go back to their homes, and we will be alone. Our friends need to celebrate. The war is over, and our family has been reunited. All is as it should be."

"But John, are *we* as we should be?"

John kissed her gently on the lips.

"We are both different people from when I left. But the one thing that was always strong in my heart was my love for you. That is not different. That has not changed."

"Thank you, John. I love you too."

She turned to the guests, who were happy. Why wasn't she? John was home to protect her, and the royal family treated Princess Anne as if she had never left.

In fact, they reveled in her distant coldness. The young princess demanded perfection from those around her, as all people born with a silver spoon in their mouths expect. Even though perfection exists only as an ideal, it is a handy way of looking down on others, pushing them away, and letting empathy shrivel like a carcass in the hot summer sun. There were moments when Anne took this behavior too far, such as casting her arrogant glances at the king or queen, but, for the most part, her behavior was accepted, and any slight was forgiven quickly. After all, she had been through a terrible ordeal at the hands of an evil witch. A period of adjustment should be expected.

Princess Anne needed no adjustment. She did not like this new "family" and longed for her room in Pesta's dark castle. Pesta taught the young princess well. Anne hated King Edward for his treachery when he took advantage of "Mother Pesta's good nature." She understood that love leads only to suffering, and no good comes from it. She hated the king's son, who killed Pesta and brought her here. She could not think of Prince John as her father. He was just like the king, black-hearted and cruel through and through. The only one she had some sympathy for was Cinderella, who was deceived, just like Pesta. And just like Pesta, there was anger inside her that could be nurtured and, with enough care, blossom into a delicate and deadly flower.

Ah, Cinderella, what could be said about Cinderella? She had lost some of her symbolic purity over the many years of waiting for her husband's return, but the common people still adored her. They no longer saw her as a symbol of hope but as a symbol of strength and resilience. She remained true to her husband. If she could remain faithful, couldn't the average citizen remain so as well?

But Cinderella remained hopeful. She used hope as a coping mechanism to survive the terrible times. When she was a girl, she hoped her father would love her as much as she knew he could.

She hoped to find true love in the arms of the prince. She hoped to find fulfillment as a mother. She hoped for her child's safety and her husband's triumphant return. And more recently, she hoped her family would find happiness together. She was willing to go into battle to make that hope a reality. She never hoped, however, for a fairytale ending. She wanted acceptance and love. The poet says, "Even if the hopes you started out with are dashed, hope has to be maintained." Another poet says, "Hope is the thing with feathers." Both might just be true.

True love is a fairy tale. It is a concept, an ideal—something to be striven for but never actually attained. If it is ever achieved, what would life be like at that moment? Does suffering go away? Does loss cease to exist? How does one survive perfection? No one could possibly know. What does perfection even look like? Maybe it is like a memory, frozen in time after the bitterness slowly fades.

Luckily, this story is not about perfect moments forever frozen in people's memories. It is a story of acceptance, love, and forgiveness. Acceptance of people who will not change for us. Love for them as they break our hearts. Forgiveness for another's weakness as we acknowledge our own imperfections.

$$\sim 4 \sim$$

The weeks after the prince's return overflowed with activity. The royals needed to regroup and plan strategy. The kingdom had just survived a war with Dandorum. King Peter died on the battlefield, and now David sits on the throne. These were unsure times. And other kingdoms sensed how vulnerable Bain was and were ready to pounce. The coffers were depleted, and raising the money would not be easy if others mounted an attack. For now, the best strategy was diplomacy.

The king raised taxes and organized huge banquets. Invitations were extended to all the neighboring kingdoms to celebrate the prince's successful quest. Kings, princes, and envoys flocked to these lavish parties. King Edward and his sons held private meetings with the visitors to show a united Bain that would remain strong even in confrontation.

Prince John happily anticipated meeting his friends from his younger days. Prince Draper of Quincy always had a bawdy joke to tell. Aliwin of Hawisa spoke a little too much and a little too loudly. Prince John wondered why he ever liked those people. But his biggest disappointment was with the princes of Zantue. They were rounder, slower, and seemed more interested in mead than participating in hunting parties. Prince John listened to their stories of bravery and horsemanship, but he could only think of Cinderella. John did not need these people as friends. He needed them to be strong allies in case of attack, and for this, the prince could listen to their empty words while lifting pints of good, strong mead.

The Queen and Cinderella met with the wives of attending dignitaries. Their job required much more subtlety than their husbands'. While the men made a show of strength, the women had to uncover weaknesses. Cinderella, however, was never comfortable with this part of her job. To manipulate others, one must be immune to manipulation. Cinderella was a little too honest for this game, but Queen Marie was a master. Princess Anne took after her grandmother.

"Look at how quickly Queen Maab averted her eyes when her husband's name came up. Their marriage is in trouble, and he is looking elsewhere. It's probably that courtesan, Albreda; she seems a bit too haughty for her place. We will have no trouble with the kingdom of Ravenna," Anne whispered into the queen's ear.

Queen Marie smiled. The princess could quickly sum up her adversaries and pinpoint their weaknesses. The years with the witch had made her hard. One day, she will be able to rule her husband and a kingdom herself. Queen Marie liked this girl.

Cinderella looked at the growing affection between the queen and Anne with concern. Although she wanted her daughter to be welcomed into the royal family, she also worried about losing the child she had so recently recovered.

King Edward's biggest concern was that King David of Dandorum did not attend any festivities. The war did not officially end; no treaties were signed. Dandorum just withdrew, leaving many neighboring kingdoms uneasy that hostilities would soon return. This new king was a mystery. David disappeared when he was just a boy and returned to kill his father and assume the throne. Who knows how this child was raised and what evil plans he was fostering? All the rest of King Edward's neighbors happily pledged their loyalty. But Dandorum was the exception. That upstart king would need to be dealt with cleverly.

~ 5 ~

Cinderella wandered through the garden. She used to spend time looking for that secluded corner where she met Evangeline. How could she have been so deceived? Trusting a stranger with the care of her young daughter? But how was she to know that Evangeline would turn out to be the witch Pesta?

Most people will forgive others before they forgive themselves, and poor Cinderella was always too hard on herself. She was isolated amongst the royals, her marriage was not the bliss that she anticipated, and the thought of raising a child in that environment overwhelmed her. This would have been daunting, even if she weren't a princess.

She thought she could somehow undo the evil that followed if she found that hidden place. But how far back would she go? Just to Evangeline? What about her marriage or even going back to the ball when she first met the prince? She had so many decisions in her life to rethink.

How many times in our lives do we sell our future to the devil? Or an evil witch? Or some fairy godmother, for that matter? Whoever it is, we give someone else the responsibility for our happiness.

She never discovered Evangeline's hiding place. So, Cinderella spent her days wandering the garden searching for Neverlands and happy endings.

"There you are," Prince John said, smiling.

"Yes, here I am." She hesitated.

"I have been looking for you."

"No search parties?" She said, recovering.

"I wanted to find you myself. Besides, I needed to get away from the Grand Duchess." He laughed.

"Oh." She turned away, disappointed.

"Oh?" He turned her around.

"Am I just an excuse to escape from a duke or duchess?"

"What is this about?"

"Nothing, it's nothing."

She walked away. John quickly stepped in front of her without touching her. She stopped but avoided his gaze, watching the grass move with the gentle breeze. He looked around, searching for something, and then he recognized it.

"Will you follow me?"

"Yes, my liege," she conceded.

They walked in silence, Cinderella following dutifully, acknowledging her place in their relationship. They soon came to a part of the garden that was less formal. Untrimmed bushes formed a barrier to the outside world. Walking through a hidden passage, Cinderella noticed the air was cooler as the trees blocked most of the sun with their large leaves. She shivered, and John put his arm around her shoulder. She involuntarily leaned her head against him.

"What is this place?" Cinderella contentedly asked.

"My parents constructed this as a playground for George and me when we were children. We had great adventures here, battling dragons and saving maidens from evil creatures."

"I had sticks on the kitchen floor," she smiled wistfully. But if I weren't careful, my stepmother would burn my toys in the hearth."

"That is so sad." He laughed gently.

She joined him. "Of course, I could gather more sticks. But no one could ever replace Sticky."

"Sticky?"

"Yes, Sticky, he was my favorite. He met a terrible end in the jaws of a neighbor's dog."

"You are joking."

"Am I joking?"

They smiled at each other. Many years had passed since they had last smiled in this way. Soon, the uneasiness returned. After a moment, Cinderella looked at her husband.

"Why am I here, John?"

"Just a moment longer," he implored, taking her hand and leading her further into the overgrown playground. His hand was rough and calloused from his battles, while her hand was soft and fragile from years of inner turmoil.

They soon arrived at a stone with a seat carved into it. The prince dusted it off and motioned for her to sit. He knelt before her.

"This was my childhood throne. Whenever I slew the dragon or some other imaginary creature, I would come home and sit on my throne while my subjects bowed at my feet. I imagined them praising my bravery. That is what I thought being a prince was all about - adventure and adoration. I met you and thought you needed rescuing. I brought you to my castle, but I abandoned you there. Then I abandoned you again to rescue another damsel in distress."

"Anne." She managed a sad smile.

"Anne," he returned her smile. "I saved our daughter, but I left you imprisoned in my castle alone. And I am sorry, Ella, with all my heart. I am sorry."

"I can't get home."

She moved to hug him, and they embraced.

"I will help you," he comforted his wife.

"I don't know whether you can," she said, her deepest fears surfacing.

"We would have to work together," he admitted. But I will do everything in my power to bring you home. I love you, Ella, with all my heart."

"You just said you were sorry with all your heart."

"I did."

"You are sorry with all your heart, and you love me with all your heart?"

"I do."

"You must have a very big heart."

"I do."

"I love you, John."

"I love you, Ella."

"Do we have to return to the duchess?"

"I don't think she has much longer in this world. We can stay a little longer."

He lay his head on her lap, and she ran her fingers through his hair. They looked over their fantasy kingdom.

"Is this what happiness is?" She asked quietly.

"I hope so," the prince smiled, closing his eyes.

The birds sang as they built their nests. Squirrels leaped from tree to tree in an aerial game of *Catch Me if You Can*. And indeed, everything in this small corner of this hidden playground seemed happy. A twig snapped under a creature's foot from deeper in the woods. The blood-red eyes looked upon the royal couple with hatred. There will be a time for the beast to attack, but not now. Soon, but not now.

~ 6 ~

Following the initial state visits from foreign dignitaries, expeditions were organized throughout the provinces for John and Cinderella to show the people that all was well. The king's subjects needed reassurance. They wanted no more battles for faraway islands or blood-soaked fields where wheat should be growing. Villages needed to be rebuilt, the dead honored, and the unnecessary pain caused by the pride of their rulers, forgotten.

Princess Anne would remain at the castle. The king thought the journey would be too much for her, and her acidic personality would not strike the right chord with the simple peasants. She needed a little more polishing before she was ready to meet her subjects. The princess welcomed the opportunity to spend more time with her grandparents and Uncle George.

Princess Anne looked out her window to the town below. There were so many people in the capital of Aristal. Pesta's castle never received any visitors, none that would live to tell about it anyway. She was a solitary witch, and although her heart was broken, Anne, deep down, thought Pesta loved her.

But the people in this horrible place showed no love, only pretense. These petty people needed to fill their empty lives with delusions, and they did this by scurrying from here to there to carry out their important business. The busy activity reminded Anne of the rats that would come out at night at Pesta's castle, except these vermin ran about in the day as well.

"May I come in?" Cinderella asked.

"If you want to mother."

"I came to say..."

"Goodbye," Anne interrupted her mother.

"Yes. I barely had a chance to say hello."

"Must you go, Mother?"

"Your father and I have some business for the kingdom."

"Then you must go."

"Yes."

"One of us always seems to be leaving."

"Yes. I'm sorry," Cinderella said.

"That's all right, Mother. I have lots of pretty things here and lots of servants to get me what I want. I probably won't even notice that you are gone."

"I hope you will. I hope you will miss me a lot."

"Yes, I will, mother, and I hope you will be miserable without me."

"I was."

"When I was with Mother Pesta?"

"Yes. Do you have to call her Mother Pesta?"

"Well, she was the only mother I remember." Anne laughed.

"I'm sorry. I should have been a better parent when you were younger."

"Nonsense. You were probably doing princess things. Just as you are doing now."

"I'm sorry. Your father and I are reassuring the people that all is well in our kingdom."

"Is everything well?"

"I hope so," Cinderella said, smiling.

"And talking to the peasants is important?"

"It can be. I was just a poor girl from a small village. I never had any fancy things, just sticks and my imagination."

"Didn't your parents give you nice things? Did they not love you?"

Anne's questions had the quality of a small child trying to figure out the world. Maybe there was no maliciousness behind the questions, but they were still painful to answer.

"I was very young when my mother died."

"You don't remember her?"

"Not as much as I would like to. Her name was Julianna. Isn't that a pretty name?" Cinderella asked.

Princess Anne shrugged and turned her gaze to the world outside her window.

Cinderella continued her memory, hoping to make a connection to her daughter. "My father would go away on business trips, and when he came back, he would happily chase me around the big willow tree in the back. My mother would stand there laughing as my father ran after me."

"Did you play such games with Father and me?" Anne turned back to her mother.

"Life in the castle is different. It is more structured and less free. I am sorry I did not play games with you when you were a child."

"Don't worry mother. I'm sure we will have lots of fun when you return."

"I hope so. I love you, Anne."

"Mother, you don't even know me," she said, smiling as she turned back to the window.

Cinderella stood there for a moment, her daughter ignoring her. She turned and left the room.

~ 7 ~

Prince John and Princess Ella enjoyed their time together while meeting their subjects. In the past, their schedule was highly structured. Every waking moment was an important ceremony, a bow, a nod, a secret meeting with a foreign dignitary to discuss a hidden subject.

Now, husband and wife could talk quietly in their carriage while they traveled. With each mile covered, they grew closer. When they arrived at their destinations, they met with small groups of excited villagers who warmly greeted the royal couple.

In truth, Prince John felt more comfortable away from the castle now. He learned so much from the people on his mission to rescue Anne about how to live happily and simply. He would trade the most extravagant state dinner for a simple meal in a small cottage with his beautiful wife any day. Cinderella felt the same but would never suggest that lifestyle to the prince. She thought he was still too tied to the castle and his obligations.

They visited many villages that were rebuilding from the war and the further away they journeyed from the capital, the more rebuilding was necessary. It is difficult for a small village to recover from an attack by a foreign army. The villagers could not raise taxes as the royalty could do to get the necessary supplies needed to restore their homes. All they could do was rebuild one house at a time, neighbor helping neighbor. It could take years, and only the most steadfast citizen chose to remain in a ravaged town. Their roots severed; most people left to find work in the capital. Many towns just faded away after a war, along with the people who lived there.

The royal couple passed through a ghost of a village called Baustimmen. All that remained of the place was a graveyard, the charred foundations of homes once occupied by happy families, and a pile of stones in the center of the town. The visitors wondered about the stones' significance.

A man approached them. He looked like a beggar, but his demeanor had an air of quiet wisdom and determination. The guards blocked his path. The prince motioned for them to let the man through.

"Who are you, sir?" Prince John asked.

"I am Tobolt, Your Majesty. I live here."

Cinderella looked around at the ruins and asked, "How can anyone live here?"

"This was my village. My wife and children and I shared that house over there," he said, pointing at a structure with one wall remaining. "King Peter's soldiers attacked us and killed everyone they could find, women and children, everyone. I was wounded and left to die in a ditch, but I didn't die, as you can see, Your Highness."

"I can see," Cinderella said, taking his hands. Tears filled her eyes. "Your name is Tobolt?"

"Tobolt, Your Majesty. Would you like to see my family?"

"Yes, Tobolt, please."

His limp made the short walk a long one. They followed the man slowly. Tobolt told of the family who lived there with every burned foundation they passed.

"This was where Thomas, the cobbler, lived. Mean as they come but was good with leather. I had a pair of his shoes, given to me by my wife on my birthday. They were taken from me as I lay dying. The soldiers recognized good workmanship. He loved Isabelle, a farmer's daughter, but she would have nothing to do with him.

His hands were too rough. Imagine that! Hands too rough for a farmer's daughter."

He stopped talking. He was standing before three graves.

"Here is my family. Catherine, Mary, and Paul. Catherine, my wife. She was a beauty. Not as pretty as you, Princess, but pretty good for our village. Black hair and brown eyes as big and bright as a full moon. We used to watch the moon, Cathy and me. We had eighty-four full moons together. That's a big number but hardly seems enough, does it?"

"No, it doesn't. Tell me about your children," said the prince, glancing momentarily at his wife.

"Mary was five and just as pretty as her mother. She wanted to be a princess one day, like you, Your Majesty. And I told her she could be if she was good and kind and looked for the good in people. She helped her mother around the house and to raise her brother. Paul was a handful. He wanted to be a brave knight and kept hitting everyone with a small wooden sword I made him, pretending they were dragons. I would chase him round and round, and he would hide behind his mother."

He stopped telling his story and looked at the boards rising from the ground with their names scratched on them. Wooden crosses were all that remained of his family.

The princess and the prince flanked Tobolt. A few steps back were the royal guards. They all looked at the graves. They had just met him, but they were now his family, his support, his tribe.

Prince John looked beyond the three graves. Many more villagers lay in shallow graves. "Did you bury everyone?"

Tobolt looked up. "No, Your Majesty, David, the prince of Dandorum, who killed his own father to end the war, passed through our village on his way home. He and his soldiers buried the dead and built the monument. Three stones for everyone in the village, one for their past, their present, and the future that was taken from them."

"Prince David, did that?" Prince John asked with a hint of suspicion.

"Yes, Your Highness."

Cinderella looked at the graves for a long time, struggling with feelings of loss and pain. "Long after a conflict has ended, the world moves on, forgetting the innocent victims who have died in lonely places. Ordinary people who have needlessly suffered are forgotten too quickly. Brave soldiers are easier to remember. Their fool hearty actions give credence to future reckless behaviors. But what about people like you, Tobolt? What of your bravery? What of your loss? You are much braver than the soldier who died in battle because your suffering came without your consent and continues long after the war has ended. I am so, so sorry, Tobolt. Come back to the castle with us, and you will live in comfort," she said.

"Thank you, Princess," he bowed to the royal couple. "But I could not leave my family."

"Then you will stay here. I will make this village a memorial to the innocent victims of the war. You will be the keeper of this monument with a royal pension. And hopefully, people will understand the cost of conflict," Prince John pledged.

"Thank you, Your Highness," Tobolt wept as he fell at their feet.

The princess helped him up and embraced him. Before leaving, the royal couple and their soldiers spent the rest of the day rebuilding Tobolt's home.

~ 8 ~

Far away from the castle, the peasant spoke to her two young children.

"Go and collect firewood for the hearth. A chill is in the air, and the night will be a cold one."

She felt the time had come for them to do chores around the house, and the mother was ready to teach them.

"Sacha, take care of Ethan."

"Yes, momma," the girl said, understanding the tremendous responsibility she was given.

"Ethan, take care of your sister," his mother said gravely.

"Yes, momma," the boy said just as gravely.

"And don't go too deep into the forest; remember what happened to the girl in the red cape."

The forest near their home was quite safe. The mother did not need to worry but wanted to put a little fear in the young ones' hearts to ensure they didn't wander too far away. The children placed one timid foot in front of the other. Danger threatened with each step! They must accomplish their task before being attacked by a big bad wolf or some other disagreeable creature.

Soon, they had forgotten all about their mother's words of warning and were happily playing as children do.

"Look at this stick. It is the best stick," said Sacha, showing her proud possession. She was always a person who wanted to get things done right. "Mommy will thank me for this stick!"

"Yeah, well, I got more sticks." Ethan countered.

"I bet this stick is a magic wand dropped by a powerful wizard killed by a brave prince."

"Tisn't," shouted Ethan.

"Tis!" said Sacha even louder.

"Tisn't!"

"Tis!"

"Tisn't"

"Tis. And I turn you into a frog. Abbacabba," she said, not knowing any magic words, but waving the stick wildly before pointing it at her brother.

The boy, pretending to be hit with a powerful magic spell, fell to the ground while throwing his collection of twigs into the air. He then sprang up and flexed his imaginary claws.

"Yes, a giant frog that likes to eat little girls!" He yelled, baring his froggy teeth.

He chased his sister as she ran deeper into the woods. She screamed, and he growled, as all giant little-girl-eating frogs do. Suddenly, she stopped. Ethan caught up to her and started playfully gnawing on her arm. When she didn't respond, he looked up.

Before the children lay a body, mauled by a beast of terrible power and size. The man, or what was left of him, rested on a palette of crimson dirt, his blood already dried on the clay earth. His carcass had been ripped and torn with tremendous ferocity, limbs separated and flung around as if delight were taken in the death of this hapless traveler. A look of terror remained on his face long after his soul had departed. Maggots feasted on the remains.

The children screamed and ran home. No longer were these woods a safe place to play out childhood fantasies, where brave knights rescue damsels in distress, and mythic quests last only until dinner. The woods were different, and so were Sacha and Ethan.

The children's mother comforted them before calling her husband from the field. He gathered several of his neighbors to find the body. No one recognized the victim. They soon concluded that he must have been an unfortunate traveler on his journey from one town to the next before meeting his fate. The men stood over the body, baffled about what animal had done this.

Then, one of the men had a strange realization. "He's not been eaten."

"What?" said the others.

"Look, there's his arm, and there's another arm. There's his right leg, and there's his left foot. He's not been eaten. He was just ripped apart."

The men looked at each other. They expected to find a body attacked by a wild boart or killed by wolves. But those beasts would have at least partially eaten their kill. Forest animals would not dismember travelers for pure pleasure. What evil had come to their forest? What evil, indeed.

~ 9 ~

The king dispatched soldiers to find the creature that killed the traveler. After several days of searching, no animal was found. The soldiers brought the remains of the victim back to the castle.

Whispers filled the crowded throne room. The body lay on a table twenty feet in front of the king. The royal surgeon examined it and reported his findings.

"Your Majesty, I know of no animal in the forest that could have done this," the doctor said, timidly. The idea that he didn't know an acceptable answer made the expert vulnerable to being replaced.

King Edward looked at the man sternly. He did not like receiving this news, especially in a filled throne room.

"What do you mean, you know of no animal that could have done this?"

"The bite marks are unusual, Your Highness. The tearing of the flesh is inconsistent with animals in this area."

"Could a bear have ripped this stranger apart?" The king asked impatiently, rapping the throne with his fingers. He needed to put an end to this quickly.

Sensing the king's growing dissatisfaction, the doctor thought it best to appease his sovereign, "I suppose so."

"What about a boart? Could a boart have torn the flesh of the poor man?"

"A boart?" The doctor repeated.

"A large boart," Edward offered.

"A large boart could have torn at his flesh."

"So, it seems you have ascertained the beast responsible for this attack, doctor. Thank you for your excellent work in solving this mystery."

The king nodded to the doctor, and the royal court politely applauded. The king had the ability to see the true nature of things and make all matters right in the kingdom. He acknowledged the accolades and motioned to the captain of his guards to approach.

"Luther, take a unit of men and find a bear or large boart that could have done this. Kill it and bring back its carcass so my subjects can see our kingdom is safe."

"Yes, Your Majesty." The captain glanced at the court smugly as if to say: *I am putting my life in danger to save my kingdom; what are you doing?*

Town criers and messengers were sent throughout the kingdom to spread the news that the king himself had dispatched soldiers to kill the dangerous creature. They should feel confident that their villages will soon be safe. The people heard his glad tidings and rejoiced. Rumors had already spread about an evil creature attacking women and young children. The beast had killed twenty people, according to recent reports, but many people were still missing.

Two weeks passed before the soldiers found an animal that could have killed the traveler. They had to journey a long distance from the castle. They passed many villages with people who could have been eaten. Yummy, rounded children to serve as tasty morsels for a hungry monster. No area that the soldiers crossed had any vicious attacks on their people. Incidents only happened in the next village over or just down the road.

Eventually, the soldiers found a large bear and lured it to its death with a deer they brought for this purpose. They let the bear eat the bait for a while so it would have blood on its jaws. Then the soldiers attacked, hitting the animal with twenty arrows. The soldiers stabbed it with their spears when it was so weakened and had no strength to defend itself.

The men returned carrying the bear's remains on a wagon. Crowds in the capital cheered their conquering heroes. They hoisted the bear up in the square outside the castle, and people marveled at how courageous the soldiers were in bringing this terrible monster to justice. Its bloody teeth and paws were proof of the animal's guilt. So, the citizens thanked the heavens for King Edward. He was a good king who put the well-being of his subjects above all else.

~ 10 ~

Cinderella felt her love for John revive. It had been years since their initial happiness sprouted like a seed, nurtured by the warmth of the sun and the cooling spring rain. He was different after his quest, more protective of the things he most cherished. She loved talking to him softly, whispering secret hopes as he held her with strength and gentleness.

John, for his part, could not believe how fortunate he was. He returned a shell of a man, and the woman he loved was waiting for him. She was changed by years of loneliness but remained faithful. Together, they would make their love blossom again, for they still loved each other and were willing to try. He could not have wished for a better outcome.

The primary purpose of their journey was to negotiate peace with Dandorum. King Edward knew of the connection Cinderella had with the new king. They were good friends, and David was willing to lay down his life for her. Edward anticipated that this would help create a lasting bond between the two kingdoms. John, however, was not apprised of David's relationship with his wife.

The royal couple stopped to rest and stretched their legs in the dark woods that bridged the kingdoms of Bain and Dandorum. Both kingdoms claimed the forest, but neither could keep it. It was a wild place, and many legends grew of magical and mysterious creatures living within its borders. Peasants avoided this area, but Prince John was accustomed to feral places from his quest. The royal couple walked ahead of their party.

The trees towered over the ground from centuries of isolation. Moss and ferns covered the forest floor. A cool crispness filled the air. Up ahead, in the path, a great stag stood. The prince went for his bow. The guards also drew their bows. What good fortune! An animal like that never casually crosses a road, and its meat would last for days. Then something occurred to the prince.

"Stop," the prince cried, holding up his hand.

The soldiers lowered their weapons. Something was familiar about this animal. The stag wasn't afraid of people. Prince John approached the animal but only got within a hundred yards before the animal bolted. He followed, racing through the thick underbrush. The guards followed the prince with Cinderella.

The animal led the prince for over an hour, finally stopping in a clearing. John stopped and looked around. This place was familiar. He watched the stag as it disappeared behind a barely visible cottage.

The group caught up with the prince, who remained motionless. Cinderella touched her husband's arm.

"What is it, John?"

"I was here while I was searching for Anne. Two brothers lived here." He walked to the structure in a daze. "We will stay here tonight," he told his men.

He pulled some vines from the front door and went in. The cottage was cold and lifeless. The brothers had died years ago.

"I was injured. Arthur and George took me in and helped me mend," he confided to his wife.

"Then I am grateful to them for taking care of you. What happened?" She asked, supporting him.

"They passed within days of each other because they could not live without each other. They spent their whole lives in these woods. Arthur was a woodsman. George was a hunter. They helped each other. They cared for each other. They completed each other."

John walked outside to the overgrown graves. He bent down and pulled up the weeds. Of course, the weeds would soon return, but he wanted the brothers to know that he loved them for their kindness and simplicity. They needed nothing but their forest and each other to be happy. They taught John many lessons about what is meaningful in life.

He stood, and Cinderella took his hand. Her hand was the only thing in his life that was necessary. They smiled at each other. So many stories to tell, but where to begin?

"One night, we sat out here just looking at the stars. We built a fire. A rabbit was roasting on the spit. I asked them if they had ever loved a girl. They were confused about the use for them," John laughed, looking at Cinderella.

"Did you enlighten them?" she laughed as well, feigning disbelief.

"I tried, although I don't think I convinced them. They asked if they both needed one. They didn't. They had each other. I was never that close to my brother or my parents. The kingdom was always the priority, and deep human connections were secondary. What good was love to the perpetuation of the kingdom? These brothers showed me that I was different from my family. I needed love. I needed your love. You are my soul, my life, my world. You opened my heart. They made me aware of how much I needed you. I am nothing without you, Ella, I am only *a walking shadow, a poor player strutting and fretting an hour upon a stage and then is heard no more.* You have given my life meaning."

~ 11 ~

A carnival atmosphere filled the square where the dead bear hung. Jugglers and musicians entertained the crowd already assembled to stare at the bloodied monster. Vendors sold fruit and vegetables to consume or throw at the carcass. Dogs and pigs hovered to catch the fallen food.

People laughed and shouted at the bear as if they could hurt it more. Young women took the opportunity to squeeze their men's arms for protection. The men happily accepted the affections of their ladies and looked around, hoping to see their friends approving this public display of affection. Older villagers shot disapproving looks at the young lovers and disgusted looks at the rotting creature before spitting on the ground and hurrying off to their busy lives. It was unclear what they found more objectionable.

Princess Anne and her entourage looked at the beast hanging from the meat hook. Several guards stood watch over the crowd to ensure the princess' safety.

Abigail, the servant girl, looked at the joy that surrounded her. She could not understand why the death of the bear brought happiness to the townspeople. "That animal did not kill that poor man, did it?" she asked the princess quietly.

"Of course not, you idiot. The peasant was dismembered, not mauled," the princess snapped. If only this horrible girl had died on the journey back to the kingdom, all would have been perfect. But Abigail remained a thorn in her side.

"But why did the king say this creature killed the traveler?"

"Because the king is weak, and the peasants are terrified. The king would rather lie to protect his power than to admit that what has come into the kingdom is beyond his power to control."

"What has come into the kingdom? Princess, I am frightened."

Anne hovered over the girl. "You are always frightened, you miserable wretch. You lack fortitude, and your weakness makes you vulnerable. Be careful that you are not the next victim."

"The next victim? You mean there will be more?"

"How do I know? Am I a fortune teller?" Anne started to raise her hand to strike the servant but thought better of it. The princess did not want another lecture from her pathetic father about being respectful to those less fortunate.

Less fortunate than herself! How could anyone be more unfortunate than she? Kidnapped from her home and forced to journey to this land of fawning and frightened beggars was almost too much to bear.

She changed her tactics with Abigail. Anne had so many ways to torture her servant; physical violence was only one method.

"Oh, there will be others. Dogs will eat the rotting bodies in the streets! No one is safe here, not even the king himself. What chance do you have?" The princess whispered threateningly.

Before the words sunk in, Anne addressed the guards, "Let us return to the safety of the castle. It seems the sight of this terrible beast has upset this servant girl. Who knows if she will be able to fulfill her duties if she stays here much longer?"

The royal party laughed at Abigail. The princess was delightful and witty. To be so positive after the ordeal she lived through spoke volumes of her courage in the face of danger. The princess turned quickly and marched back to the safety of the castle, followed by the guards and her entourage.

Abigail stood staring at the bear. A sudden storm came upon the town. The darkness and rain dissipated the crowd, but Abigail remained. Her tears were hidden by the rain running down her face. She could not tell whether the tears were from empathy for the murdered creature or from fear of what would happen next. Maybe it was a little of both.

Soldiers cut down the creature after a week. The carcass started to smell, and the people knew they were safe. After another week, the terrible attack was forgotten, and everyone went back to their quiet, ignorant lives.

~ 12 ~

"Your Majesty, the delegation from Bain has passed through the village of Tinbet and should be here within the hour," the messenger told King David.

The king looked to his mother, Queen Anast, on his right, and William Valdman, his trusted friend and advisor, on his left. His eyes narrowed.

"Who is in this delegation?"

"Prince John back from his quest to find his daughter and Princess..."

"Ella," the king finished the messenger's sentence.

"Yes, Your Highness," the messenger bowed.

"Thank you. Have the steward prepare the guest apartments for their arrival."

"Yes, Your Highness," he bowed again and exited.

"Why have they come?" Queen Anast fumed. "They killed your father, and now they want concessions."

"I killed my father, Mother," David said quietly.

"You didn't know," she pleaded, never fully accepting the truth.

"I don't know whether that would have changed anything," his tone remained measured and distant. "Please leave us and prepare for their arrival."

"Yes, sire." She knew her place since her husband's death.

Valdman spoke when the queen had gone. "They sent Cinderella."

"Yes."

"King Edward knows her power over you."

"That was a lifetime ago, William."

"You were ready to lay down your life for her."

"I was ready to lay down my life for you if I remember."

"Women are different, Your Majesty."

"Are they, William?" David smiled at his friend.

Valdman realized he was arguing his point a little too forcibly. He returned the smile to his king. "Yes, they are, Your Majesty. Princess Ella was sent here to exploit your weakness. All I am advising is that you remain cautious."

"I will be. People say Prince John has been trained well by his father. Let us see what is requested. We withdrew from the battle. We did not surrender. Our kingdom is strong but not foolish. I doubt they want to continue this aggression."

~ 13 ~

Aristal, the capital of Bain, was quiet. As tomorrow was the Lord's Day, most people were at home with their families, thinking of church. This was a religious city. The three spires of the cathedral dominated the city's skyline, which, in the moonlight, looked kindly down on the people it protected. In the Malbet market, one of the smaller markets in town that specialized in carved wooden figures of holy men and housewares, the sellers packed their goods with the setting sun. A few stragglers talked with their neighbors about how successful the day had been. Beggars carefully checked the empty stalls for items left behind. The vendors, knowing this, left a little something for the poor.

Alard, the Potter, looked at his almost empty cart. He had done particularly well that day. He smiled, looking past his long journey home to his meeting with Warin, the silk merchant, after church the next day. Warin was also doing well with his ship coming in last month and wanted to tile the walls of his shop to show off his good fortune. This would bring Alard the comfort he always desired. He might even be able to take a wife, one with a little extra weight on her, so people would think Alard could take care of his woman.

Though Alard did well that day, the empty streets at night always made him uncomfortable. After the sun had set, all sorts of unsavory people came out. He kept his mind on pleasant thoughts as he walked down the quiet streets. Soon, he would be sitting in front of a warm fire in his home.

He heard a dog's growl behind him, but when he turned around, the street was empty. A few moments later, he heard the sound again. After seeing nothing, he quietly took the stick from his cart and walked towards the sound.

"Shoo, shoo, away with you," he shouted, but only silence answered.

He put the stick back on his cart and remembered the leftover meat and a roll he hadn't finished earlier because he was so busy. Well, maybe he could get the dog to leave him alone by throwing it the scraps of food. He tossed the leftovers on the street and started his journey at a quicker pace.

A moment later, the sounds returned, and Alard had had enough. He grabbed his weapon and moved quickly down the side street where the animal was hiding. As soon as he turned the corner, he dropped the stick. This was no dog. The thing was bigger, much bigger, and its growl was deeper and angrier. The beast rose to full height, towering over poor Alard. The terrified man tried to scream, but the sound stuck in his throat. The creature moved in for the kill, biting the man's neck and severing his head from the rest of his body, which fell limp as the animal drank the blood on the cobblestone street.

The next morning, a priest came out of the cathedral to sweep the steps for the parishioners arriving soon. A person who must have had too much to drink the night before slept on the steps. This was not unusual, and the priest jovially approached the person.

"Friend, it is time for morning prayers. Come in and have something to eat before the services begin."

As the priest approached, he sensed the person wasn't peacefully sleeping off a drunken night. He saw that the body was headless. He looked out into the deserted square. The shadow from the cathedral filled areas in darkness. The priest no longer felt safe.

Before entering the cathedral to alert the bishop, he crossed himself and looked to heaven for protection.

Soldiers from the castle soon arrived. The victim, whoever he was, was not robbed. His money purse still hung from his belt. Later in the day, it was discovered the victim was Alard the Potter when his cart was found in the market district. A child discovered his head several streets from his cart.

This was not a robbery. This was something darker. The way poor Alard was dragged, headless, through the streets to be thrown on the steps of the cathedral seemed to warn the people of Bain that no one was safe.

By the time churchgoers started arriving, word had spread throughout the capital of another murder. People connected this gruesome death with the poor traveler in the woods. They wondered if the creature had been caught, as the king promised. They wondered if whatever was in the dark woods a month ago was now in the city. And the people were right in their concern.

$$\sim 14 \sim$$

"**W**elcome, Bain, to the court of Dandorum," King David said without rising, looking directly at Prince John.

The throne room was filled with courtiers in a display of pomp and power. David was in his own court and wanted to show it.

"Greetings, King David. We have come because we believe there can be peace between our kingdoms," John said, not breaking David's gaze.

Cinderella took a step forward and bowed. She looked up and recognized her friend. She knew of David's escape but nothing of his rise to the throne. She did not know that he was King Peter's long-lost son, nor was she aware of his part in the death of his own father.

A slight gasp escaped her mouth, and then she smiled broadly before realizing where she was. She could hardly contain her excitement. David was a king, and this was his kingdom. She was only a visiting dignitary from a foreign land and must maintain decorum.

David looked at her and smiled slightly. John noticed the king's change in demeanor and his wife's surprise. Valdman, who was by the king's side, saw everything as well.

"Hello, Ella. You look well," the king's familiarity was intentional.

"Thank you, Your Majesty. You look much better than the last time I saw you," she could not help but smile at her friend.

"Yes, King Edward wanted my head on a platter." He looked back at John.

John was visibly troubled. He was not aware that his wife and the king knew each other.

"John," Cinderella said, taking his arm and reassuring him, "before David was a king, he was a kitchen boy at our castle."

"I am glad you were able to rise from such humble beginnings, Your Highness," John said lightly, trying to recover.

"It seems as if you were unaware of the friendship I've had with your wife. There may be a better time to discuss matters of state. Please retire to your rooms and settle in. It appears as if you and your wife have much to talk about. We will continue our discussions after dinner."

He motioned to a servant who immediately approached the royal couple to show them to their rooms. John bowed and sharply extended his arm to Cinderella, who took it. She sensed his anger. They turned quickly and followed the servants.

"Do you think it wise to antagonize the prince, Your Highness?" Valdman whispered so the court would not hear this chastisement.

David smiled at his subjects and leaned toward his friend. "No, I don't believe it was, but I was humiliated in Edward's court. I want John to understand whom he is dealing with."

"Did Prince John wrong you?"

"Did I wrong him?" David asked sharply.

"No, Your Highness. But a jealous husband is not someone you can trust with his word."

"I understand, but I believe the prince will do what is in the best interest of Bain."

"She still has power over you, David." Valdman was not talking to the king as an advisor but as his friend. "I saw the way she looked at you and how you looked at her. Do you still have feelings for her?"

"I believe I do."

"And now Prince John knows that as well."

"We will use that to our advantage. But he must know we approach negotiations from a position of power," David said, leaning back on the throne and smiling at his court.

"Hopefully, this will not cause further animosity between the kingdoms," Valdman said, returning to his role as advisor. He remained concerned about his king's tactics but would follow his friend to the end.

~ 15 ~

After poor Alard's death, people in the capital were frightened. This was not the death of a stranger miles away from the city. One of their own was brutally murdered without reason. Alard was a good man with no enemies and did not deserve this fate.

King Edward could not send soldiers into the forest to kill another bear to calm the tension in the capital. Each day, his subjects came to the castle to get reassurance that they were safe. But what could he say? This was not a foreign invader. Edward could not raise taxes, train an army, and vanquish the enemy in battle. He did not know what this was and was ill-prepared to deal with it.

He was a king. And kings organize campaigns. He instituted a curfew in the city. Everyone needed to be in their homes by sundown. After this time, anyone caught in the streets would be considered a suspect and arrested. The dungeon quickly filled with beggars and drunkards. The king's actions did not stop the disquiet, and the crowds outside the castle became angrier. The people were losing faith in their king.

Vigilante groups formed in each district of the city to patrol their areas. Several days before, one of these groups attacked a couple coming from a tavern. This caused more unrest, and soldiers were sent to calm the citizens. A few ruffians were arrested. Their group was broken up, but a few days later, the group reformed and began patrolling the streets again.

"The rabble is stupid and afraid," Princess Anne said, secretly delighting in the chaos as she looked from her window to the town below. "Mother Pesta was right. They deserve to be wiped from the world."

"They just want a happy life, Princess," Abigail said softly.

"What did you say?" Anne growled, turning her gaze from the capital to her servant.

The servant lowered her voice even more. "They just want to be happy."

"Happiness! What is happiness? It is a tool of the monarchy to keep the commoners in their place. It would be better for them to pray for the power to control their own fate. So, there is a creature attacking them. Let one of them rise up, kill the beast, and become a hero. Or better yet, let the people rise up and overthrow the tyrant that rules them."

"That tyrant is your grandfather."

"He is a tyrant just the same. Do you remember what he did to our Mother Pesta? She wanted happiness, and he destroyed her for it. Now he has grown old and weak, and the evil he has brought into the world has come home to roost."

"What are you saying, Anne?"

"I have grown tired of talking to you."

"Please, please, Anne, I beg you, what will happen?"

"Are you afraid for your life? Don't worry; no harm will come to you as long as you keep to your place. Now get out." The princess grabbed a goblet from the dressing table and flung it at the girl, striking Abigail in the head. Abby fell to the ground unconscious. The smile on Anne's face faded. She touched her head as she lost consciousness as well.

"Oh, Mother Pesta, what have you done?" She gasped before falling beside her servant.

~ 16 ~

King David's servants quietly finished preparing the room for the visiting royals and then left them. The silence remained. Cinderella finally spoke.

"I'm sorry, John. I should have told you that David and I knew each other. But I did not know this David was the person I knew."

"Yes, you should have," he turned away, looking out the small window in the room. "How did you know each other?"

"We were friends."

"And how does a princess become friends with a kitchen boy?" he said, trying to contain his anger.

"He made a particularly good soup. I came down to the kitchen one night. He was trying out recipes. I was hungry, and he fed me. We talked about things. We became friends."

"Why would you talk to a servant about things?"

"You forget where I came from."

"I didn't forget, but a certain propriety must be maintained."

"Did you maintain that propriety when we met?"

"No, I didn't."

"And if you did maintain that propriety, would we be married?"

"No," the prince said quietly.

"John, would you have preferred that?" She looked into his eyes.

"No, Ella, you are the most important person in my world." They looked at each other for a moment before he asked tentatively, "Would you have preferred that?"

"John, dearest John, you are the most important person in the world to me as well."

They held each other tightly, sensing how close their relationship was to ending. A diversion of their eyes or a moment's hesitation might have destroyed their marriage, but they seemed to survive for the moment.

Cinderella was relieved that her friendship with David was now in the open. She would have no further secrets from her husband.

John sensed a distance from his wife on his return. He believed it was because he had changed, but maybe Cinderella had changed as well.

On his quest, John met many different people. They transformed his ideas and became his friends. How could he deny Cinderella's friendships as well? But husbands tend to be jealous, especially if wives keep their friendships a secret.

"And what did you talk about with this servant?"

"We talked about you. He gave me hope you would return one day with Anne. He gave me strength."

"Couldn't my mother or father have given you that strength? Couldn't George?"

"John, the only thing that your parents did for me was to make me feel small and isolated. Have they ever made you feel differently?"

"They were preparing me to become king one day. I had to be strong. Comfort and understanding from others make a ruler fragile."

"To empathize with others gives you compassion and humility. It makes you a better person and a better king," she said, approaching her husband and stroking his face. "I can assure you, my liege and my husband, we were friends. That is all."

John held his wife at a distance, "So why would my father want to kill him?"

"Your brother painted the picture of impropriety out of jealousy. When they could prove nothing, David was accused of being a spy. He was not a spy but accepted the punishment to spare my reputation. That is what a friend and an honorable man would do. The last time I saw him was at the trial. David managed to escape, and I am glad he did. He did not deserve that treatment."

John thought for a moment. He had to believe his wife if there was to be any hope of their love surviving. His love kept him alive in the darkest days of his quest. It would be wrong if he would allow his suspicions to kill his love now. He believed his wife.

"Ella, it is hard for me to learn of your friendship in such a way. I think of how lonely and isolated you must have been. I think about the secrets you told a servant because I was not around, secrets that you should have told me. That is difficult for a man."

"It is difficult for me as well. But John, we have our whole life together. What words David and I shared at night in the kitchen will pale to what you and I will share in the future. We need to trust each other. I love you, John, and have from our first moment together and will to my last breath. I will always love you."

"I love you too, Ella."

"Thank you." She smiled at her husband.

"You're welcome," he said, embracing his wife.

They held each other for a long time. Maybe there was hope for them. Just maybe.

~ 17 ~

A soft knock came from the other side of the door. The person waited anxiously for a response. Another knock, this time a little louder.

"Princess, it is time to prepare your bed," said Celeste, the worried servant.

She slowly opened the door to see Anne and Abigail on the floor. She ran to the princess and turned her over, cradling the girl in her arms.

"Get the physician. The Princess is ill," she called to the empty doorway, hoping someone would hear.

Immediately, five servants appeared. Four of them helped the princess to her bed, and the last one ran to get help.

Simon, a guard, appeared at the door. "What happened here?" he demanded.

"I don't know. I came to turn down the bed and found them on the floor," answered Celeste.

"Them?"

"Princess Anne's girl was also on the floor."

"Blood is on the girl's head," the guard said, examining Abigail. "She must have received this wound defending the Princess from an attacker."

"Lord, have mercy on us," cried one of the servants.

"An attacker in the castle?" cried another just as loud.

Several more guards appeared in the doorway.

"Protect the Princess while I find the captain. There's an intruder in the castle!" Simon said, dashing off.

The guards drew their swords. The servants huddled around the princess.

Abigail opened her eyes and slowly sat up on the floor where the servants had left her. The guards turned their weapons on her. Abigail cried out in fear. Mary, an older housekeeper, pushed through the soldiers.

"Sod off, you idiots. You think this girl is the attacker?" Mary snapped, helping Abigail to a chair. "Are you all right, chicken?" she asked kindly.

Abigail smiled at Mary. She had never been called a chicken before and hoped Mary was being friendly. However, she was disoriented, so she could not be sure.

"I think I am all right."

"Celeste found you and the princess on the floor. What happened, dear?"

Quince, one of the guards, stepped forward, "That is enough from you. This is a criminal matter," he barked at the servants, waving his sword around. "What happened here?" he demanded. The servants moved away from Mary and Abigail to an unoccupied corner of the room.

The Captain of the Guard appeared at the door. "What is going on here?" he ordered.

The guards stepped away from Quince and moved to a different corner of the room, unoccupied by the servants.

"I do not know, sir. I was in the process of questioning the witnesses," stammered the deserted guard.

"Well then, let me talk to the girl," the captain said, stepping with large strides into the room as Quince retreated.

"What is going on here?"

Everyone in the room turned to the princess sitting up in bed. They took a step towards her. Anne glared at everyone, and they all retreated in unison.

"Why are you here?" she hissed.

"I came because I was summoned. You were attacked," the Captain of the Guard sputtered.

"What kind of dunce are you? Who summoned you?" the princess bellowed.

"He did," the captain said, pointing at Simon.

Anne rose from the bed, "Are you all idiots? I don't know whether to imprison or execute every one of you. Did you see an attacker?"

"No, Your Majesty," Simon said, wishing he wasn't the first soldier on the scene. "She found you unconscious, and there was blood on your maid's head," he explained nervously, pointing to Celeste.

"Did you see an attacker?" the irate princess screamed at Celeste.

"No, no, Your Majesty. I knocked to turn down the bed, and when you did not answer, I opened the door to find you and Abigail on the floor. Then I called for help."

"Does it look like I need your help?" she barked. No one dared answer the angry princess. "Does it?"

They timidly looked at their boots, not responding.

"No! I thought so. Now get out!"

The Captain of the Guard cautiously stepped forward. "I'm sorry, Princess, but I cannot withdraw until I know what happened here. I need to know if there is an intruder in the castle."

"Get out!"

"I'm sorry, Princess," he said, standing his ground.

The princess looked as if she were about to explode. She walked over and picked up the goblet from the floor. "You see this goblet? I threw it at this stupid girl because she was not quick enough to respond to a command. Then I slipped on the spilled wine. Now get out," she wailed, throwing the goblet at the captain.

He deflected the chalice, which hit Timothy, another soldier with the bad fortune of standing beside the captain. The servants followed the guards out of the room. Only the princess and Abigail remained.

Celeste stuck her head back in the room, "Excuse me, Princess, but do you want your bed turned down now?"

The princess glared at her, and Celeste disappeared. Anne went to the door and locked it so they would not be interrupted. She turned to Abigail, who looked around for help from the empty room.

"What happened before?"

"What do you mean?" Abigail asked, afraid of what the princess would do to her.

"You know what I meant. When I knocked you out, I fell down as well."

"I don't know," she cried, curling herself into a ball to make herself as small as possible.

"Yes, you do. What did Mother Pesta do to us?" Her anger was rising.

"I don't know," Abigail pleaded.

Anne pulled the servant from the chair. "I swear I will throw you from the window if you don't tell me the truth."

"If you do, what will happen to you?"

"What," said the princess, still threatening the girl.

"You threw the goblet at me, and when I fainted, you fell as well. What do you think will happen to you if you killed me?"

"I don't know," Anne said, loosening her grip on Abigail.

"You would surely die, Princess. You would die."

"She enchanted us?"

"I think she might have," Abigail said, hoping not to be beaten.

Anne let Abigail go in disgust. She paced around the room. Abigail curled back into a ball in the chair from which she had been pulled moments before.

"Why would Mother Pesta do that to me? How could she do this to me?"

"Maybe she didn't want you to kill me."

"Why not?"

"I don't know."

The princess stopped pacing and looked at the girl she took great delight in abusing. She would no longer be able to beat this servant with the same exuberance as she had in the past, which made her sad.

"Does that mean you would die as well if I died?" Anne finally said softly.

"I don't know, Princess."

"Does that mean if you killed me, you would die also?"

"Why would I kill you, Your Highness? I am bound to keep your secrets, and you, safe," Abigail began feeling frightened again.

"Maybe it was a coincidence, my losing consciousness. I should throw you out the window to test that idea."

She grabbed the servant again and moved towards the window.

"Please, please, Princess. I don't know why this is happening, but maybe Pesta wanted us to depend on each other. To care and protect each other."

Anne threw the girl to the floor and began pacing again. If Pesta bound them together, there must be a reason. But why? She hated being dependent on another person, especially this weak and fawning servant. She wanted to kill her just because she couldn't. She wanted to scream and throw things. She needed to get away before she hurt Abby. She headed for the door.

"Where are you going?" Abigail asked nervously.

"Stay here if you know what is good for you. I don't know whether we had a spell put on us, but I will test that theory if you follow me."

The princess slammed the door as she left. Abigail curled back into a ball, afraid to move from the chair.

~ 18 ~

The full moon shone brightly on the cool, clear night as the church bells struck one. A gang of drunken rowdies hid as the king's soldiers passed on patrol. They had been drinking since they had been released from the king's dungeons hours before.

They reveled in being arrested for being out after curfew because they saw themselves as a citizen's patrol, protecting the city from unknown evils stalking the streets at night. Even though groups like this one were ill-prepared for actual confrontation, they comforted people and protected the streets, if only because they made so much noise that ordinary criminals sought quieter places to carry on their business.

The citizen's patrol roamed the streets until they were too drunk or tired to continue. Then they would stumble home and wake their wives and children as they bumped into the furniture, trying to find their welcoming beds.

A cloud passed over the moon, blackening the streets when the drunken patrol came upon the gruesome scene. A creature stood over a group of bodies visible only by the ring of torches that, moments before, were carried by the fallen men. Ten soldiers lay dead in the street, blocks from the castle's gates.

The citizen's patrol dropped their weapons, and the beast turned quickly to the intruders. Its blood-red eyes reflecting the dying flames quickly scanned the drunken men. A low growl of delight and anger emerged from deep within its dark soul. Moments later, it pounced upon the first man, severing his neck. The others, no longer in a laughing mood, ran down the street screaming for help. But the beast was too swift for them, picking them off one by one. The monster caught the last man near the main castle gate, grabbing him from behind and flipping him over.

"Hey, what is going on there?" a soldier demanded from up on the castle walk.

The beast turned to the lookout. It leaped at the wall, but the barrier was too high to scale. It tried a second and third time, growing angrier, finally howling in frustration.

"Help, help, come quick," the soldier cried to his fellow men in arms, disappearing from the beast's sight behind the wall and sounding more like a frightened child than a member of the king's guard.

Others appeared quickly with bows pointed at the creature. Before they could shoot, it disappeared into the darkness.

The soldiers carried the wounded man into the castle. It was too late to save him. He swore his attacker was no forest animal but an enchanted spirit, half man and half beast. No mortal being could defeat such a wicked thing. He died with a look of terror still in his eyes.

A troop of soldiers was sent to recover the bodies before sunrise. The Captain of the Guards did not want more hysteria in the capital. They proceeded slowly, following the line of bodies back to the squad of dead soldiers like a trail of breadcrumbs in a fairytale.

The dead soldiers were all battle-worthy, having fought in the war against King Peter. But their attacker moved so quickly they could not even unsheathe their swords.

The king and queen were awakened when the bodies were safe within the castle. Ten soldiers and six vigilantes lay in the chapel, overcrowding the small sanctuary. The king was visibly shaken. He was a man of war. But this was not a war with clear battle lines or combatants holding different colored flags. There was no pomp and circumstance here, only death.

"Bring the Bishop to pray for these poor souls," he directed the captain of the guard.

"Yes, Your Highness. We will also search the castle to ensure everything is secure," the soldier said, trying to reassure his king.

"Thank you."

Soldiers surrounded the chapel to protect the king and queen. One went to wake Princess Anne and bring her to safety.

The next day, the king sent word to Prince George, who was discussing trade in the kingdom of Tansic, to remain in place and in safety. He called for John and Cinderella to return, hoping the royal couple could bring calm to Bain.

~ 19 ~

After the evening meal, Cinderella spent time with Queen Anast while the men discussed matters of state.

A servant escorted Prince John into the library, where he found King David talking in hushed tones with his advisor, William Valdman.

"Thank you, William. I believe I can entertain the prince for a while," he said lightheartedly.

"Yes, Your Highness." Valdman bowed to the king and then to the prince before taking his leave.

"Did you enjoy dinner? I apologize for my absence," King David shrugged. "But important state business needed my attention."

David sat on a chair at the head of the table, scattered with books. He motioned for John to join him. John sat opposite him.

"The queen was a delightful hostess. I hope your business came to a favorable conclusion. I appreciate your concern," Prince John assured the king.

David did not need any assurance. The state business was an excuse for not dining with his guests. Prince John, taught well by his father, recognized this childish deception as a negotiation tactic.

"And the princess? Is she comfortable with the arrangements?"

"Yes, we are quite comfortable. Thank you."

"I am pleased to hear that," David said.

"I must say that I am not comfortable with your friendship with my wife during my absence. It does not seem appropriate for royalty."

"I was not a royal when I was friends with your wife," David replied. "But only a lowly kitchen boy."

"You were born a royal and will always be one, no matter the circumstances."

"Nothing in life is certain. Each path is perilous and is laden with pitfalls. You can be king one day and a beggar the next," David said, speaking from experience.

"And become a king the day after that," John countered. "I am uncomfortable with your friendship with my wife, but it was important to her at the time, so I thank you for that."

"You are welcome. But you are not here to forgive me for my imaginary transgressions. You have come to discuss a cessation of hostilities between our kingdoms."

"You are correct, Your Highness," John said, slightly bowing his head.

"I have no desire to continue a war between Dandorum and Bain," David casually offered. "It seems to be more of a concern of our father's generation than our own."

"I agree."

"But your father is still sitting on the throne, a position you may never attain. What would prevent him from restarting hostilities?" David was on the attack again, leaning into his opponent.

"Hostilities began when your father attempted the unlawful seizure of land in my kingdom."

David sat back in his seat, smiling like a cat toying with a mouse before the end. "That is what rulers do. Your father taught me that when I tended to him on the battlefield. Did you know that?"

John's eyes narrowed. He would not be distracted. "No, I did not. This trip has revealed a wealth of information I was not acquainted with. I am in your debt for many things which do not influence our discussion. You withdrew from the battle. Hopefully, that means you do not desire to resume."

"I have not decided."

John rose from his seat. He had had enough of this frivolousness. He came to this king to stop the bloodshed, but this petty boy seemed more interested in playing games.

"David, it seems to me that you are too immature to rule a country. Throwing an inappropriate relationship with my wife in my face. Missing dinner to make me uncomfortable shows the impetuousness of a child. You are a king. You hold the destinies of your subjects in your hands. Our fathers seemed to have forgotten that fact, but you and I are different. We've spent time with our people and have seen their struggles. We have stood in villages wiped out on whims. Ella and I passed through Baustimmen on our way here. We met Tobolt, who lost his family when your father's army attacked without provocation or mercy. On your return to Dandorum, you helped bury those innocent victims. I know what you thought of the war. I believe our kingdoms can live in peace and grow wealthy together."

"My chief advisor and friend, William, similarly lost his family," the king said, remembering why he had joined his enemy to fight his father.

"How many others will have similar fates as their rulers move armies around like pieces on a chess board?"

"That is what rulers do," David said, now sounding less confident in his words.

"But we could be different."

"Are you sure, John?"

"I hope so."

The king looked up and noticed a servant standing in the doorway.

"Yes, what is it?"

"A message for Prince John from King Edward, my liege," the servant said, bowing deeply.

The king held out his hand to receive the letter but immediately passed it to Prince John as a sign of respect. The prince read it and handed it back to the king.

"Regretfully, Your Highness, it seems that I have urgent state business at home," he said, smiling as he recognized the irony of the situation.

King David warmly smiled in return. He knew that the kingdoms had not yet concluded their treaty. What could be more important than that?

"We are not done with our business, but I trust this is not a manipulation for advantage. I hope what you have told me tonight is true, and I will proceed as such. With your permission, William Valdman will accompany you to Bain to conclude the business between our two countries. He is more thoughtful and less impetuous than I am, so you will have a harder time with him than with me. Please say goodbye to Princess Ella for me."

"Thank you, Your Highness," John said. "I hope to meet again one day on a more social occasion."

The prince left quickly to arrange his departure. The king signaled to his servant.

"Please tell the queen to release Princess Ella to her husband and send Valdman to me."

$$\sim 20 \sim$$

The guard knocked on Princess Anne's door. Abigail had not moved since the princess stormed out. Startled by the loud knock, she slowly approached the door. Surely, the princess would not bother to knock before entering. Who could this be?

"Who's there?" she asked, barely above a whisper.

"Timothy, one of the castle guards. Something has happened, and we need the Princess to come to the great hall where she will be protected."

Abigail looked at the empty bed and then back to the door. She did not like to lie but could see no way around it.

"She is sleeping. I am sure she will be safe. Please go away."

"I am sorry, but this is an order from the king. I must insist you open the door."

The poor girl panicked. She ran to the bed and rumpled the covers before opening the door for the guard. He strode in and looked around. Abigail recognized him as the guard who was hit by the goblet earlier.

"Where is the Princess?" he asked, both relieved and suspicious.

"She is changing."

"I thought you said she was sleeping."

"She was before you knocked."

"Shouldn't you be helping her?"

"Yes, but I couldn't open the door if I were dressing the princess in the other room. Could I?" Abigail smiled before going into the other room.

He smiled back at her, embarrassed at his stupidity. After she left, he rubbed the bump on his head.

Abigail's smile faded when she left the soldier's sight. What was she going to do? What was she going to do? She said that question quietly, as Pesta would speak while conjuring as if the answer would magically appear. Miraculously, she got a favorable response from the universe.

"What are you doing here?" Princess Anne demanded.

"What are you doing there?" the bewildered guard answered, pointing at the door the princess had just entered from.

"What are you talking about? Where is my servant?"

"She is dressing you in there," he said, motioning to the room Abigail was hiding in.

Anne realized that this was Abigail's feeble attempt to cover for her. Her mood changed, and she addressed the soldier kindly.

"Why are you here?"

"Something has happened, and we need you to come to the great hall for protection."

"You can't protect me here?" she cooed at the soldier.

"It is the command of the king," he said, lowering his guard.

"You were here earlier. What is your name?" She gently touched the bump on his forehead.

"Timothy, Your Highness."

"Did I do this to you, Timothy?"

"I'm sure it was an accident. You were aiming at the captain of the guard."

"I was, wasn't I? Timothy, would you mind waiting outside while I talk to my idiot servant? It appears she doesn't know whom she is dressing in the other room."

"Yes, ma'am," Timothy said sheepishly.

When the door closed, the princess turned to the room Abigail was hiding in.

"Abigail, do you mind coming out here?"

The servant nervously entered the room, not knowing what to expect but expecting the worst.

"Yes, Your Highness."

Abigail stopped in front of the princess and lowered her head. Anne lifted the girl's chin, and she pulled away. Abigail was not used to being touched kindly by the princess. Anne smiled at the response, although it was not unexpected.

"There, there, Abigail. I am not going to strike you. Did you tell the guard that I was dressing?"

Anne's gentle tone did nothing to calm her servant.

"Yes."

"And what would have happened if I had not arrived when I did? Would you have stayed there all night?"

"Yes."

"My, I am a leisurely dresser," Anne said with a hint of sarcasm.

"Yes."

"You lied for me, Abigail. And I thank you for that. It would have been awkward if you did not do so. Mother Pesta was right in forcing me to keep you around."

"Thank you, " Abigail said with a sigh of relief. She touched a bruise on her arm from a previous beating from the princess. After a moment, her tone changed. "But where were you, Princess? Something has happened, and you could have been in danger."

Anne turned and walked away from her servant. The happy moment between the two evaporated. Was this girl accusing her of something? She turned to punish the girl, anger in her eyes, but then consciously softened her tone. This was not the time to deal with her servant's suspicion.

"After you upset me, I walked around the castle until I was hungry. I went to the kitchen to get something to eat. Does that satisfy you?" Anne asked as if she were speaking to a child.

"I am sorry, Princess. I did not mean to upset you."

"That is fine, Abigail. But let us keep that a secret. No need to worry the king and queen with trivialities in these terrible times."

"Of course, Your Highness," she said dutifully, but deep down, doubting that the princess had told her the truth.

~ 21 ~

These were difficult times in Bain, as if a dark cloud had hung over the kingdom. Fear of the unknown grew unrestrained, and peace, starved of nourishment, was like a flower in a drought, left to shrivel and die.

Estrilda was a healer. She worked with herbs, berries, leeches, and spiders to bring her patients to health. Ever since she was young, the old woman understood the nature of a body's illness. Her hand would pass over the weakened person until she reached a point where the heat of the illness focused her attention. Then, she would work her magic.

She used leeches and botanicals for many problems, but she had a way with spiders. Estrilda could extract the venom from her larger spiders. She made a paste for the smaller arachnids, which attracted the creatures to where they needed to inject their poison, bringing the patient back to health.

She traveled from town to town in her wagon, helping people. Her customers were grateful but uneasy around her. Estrilda's age and wild appearance gave the impression that hidden forces assisted her. She did not mind the way people thought of her. After all, who would not pay a witch?

She enjoyed helping people get better and bringing news before official word came from the capital. She told some outlying villages about the end of the war with Dandorum and of Prince John's happy return. Now that her journeys had taken her closer to Aristal, she anticipated hearing the latest gossip.

The village of Valpechi was typical, with two dozen houses huddled around the road leading to the capital. At the end of town was a slightly larger house that served as a tavern, having a few rooms for travelers. Most people in the village were poor farmers. As Estrilda slowly passed through on her wagon, the children ran back to their homes frightened, calling to their mothers, who looked scornfully at the stranger. Usually, they would be more welcoming, even to one as wild-looking as Estrilda, but the place where the traveler had been killed was only down the road.

A villager caught up with her just after she passed the tavern. "Estrilda, my child has taken ill. Please help her," he pleaded, running beside her cart.

The woman stopped and looked at the man. He seemed familiar, "I believe I helped your wife during childbirth. Your name is Samir," she said as if calling on the powers from beyond.

"Savaric, ma'am. The very child that you helped bring into the world is now sick. Please, can you help her?"

Of course, she would help the man, but she wanted to look as if she were pondering the mysteries of the heavens so he would think she was on some particularly important business. After a moment, she smiled a toothy grin and said, "Climb on."

During the trip to his house, Savaric explained how the pain in his daughter's knees was so bad she could hardly stand. When they arrived, they found the young girl in bed crying.

"Emma, you remember Estrilda," the man said to his wife, making quick introductions.

"Of course, thank you for helping our daughter," the mother said anxiously.

Estrilda sat on the bed and held the child's hand, who immediately stopped crying at the stranger's touch.

"You are cold, my dear," said Estrilda, smiling at the child.

"We have kept her near the fire, but nothing seems to warm her," Emma said, clutching her husband, a little afraid of the visitor.

Estrilda removed the blanket and placed her hands slightly above the girl's knees. She closed her eyes and exhaled slowly, pushing as much air from her lungs as possible. Her magic seemed to work better when she was almost out of breath. Then she stopped her breathing, and in that small moment between exhaling and inhaling, her vision became clear. The delayed pause ended suddenly with a deep breath, which frightened the parents, who held each other close. Estrilda's head dropped, and she remained silent for several long moments. The girl's parents were close to tears, unaware of the meaning of this strange behavior.

Finally, the old woman stood up slowly and looked into the couple's eyes.

"Your daughter is very sick because her humours are trapped."

"What?" asked the mother.

"The body has four humours: blood, yellow bile, black bile, and phlegm. Their balance in the body ensures health. Too much black bile in the child above the knees. This is the reason she is cold there. Her blood is blocked in her knees. That is causing her fever."

"Will she be alright?" the worried father asked.

"Unless we can get her humours to balance, she will surely die," the healer predicted.

The wife cried into her husband's chest, "What can be done to save her?"

"Spider venom can unblock her fluids, but it is not sure," Estrilda explained.

"Whatever you can do, Estrilda, we will pay you what we can."

The healer smiled and said, "Then let us begin."

She headed to her wagon. By this time, the neighbors had gathered around the house. They disliked strangers, especially evil-looking ones. The healer waved her hands, shooing the nosy villagers away while she got to work.

She disappeared behind the canvas covering of her wagon. The villagers closed in tightly to hear what magical spells the witch was conjuring. When they heard shrieks and curses, they backed away. Estrilda could not find the right spiders for her remedy and cursed the spirits for hiding them. The wagon's flap suddenly opened, and the villagers scattered. Estrilda emerged smiling with two jars in her hands; one had the Yorik spiders from deep in the dark forest, and the other hand had the potion that would attract the spiders to the intended spot.

Estrilda sneered at the ignorant villagers. She knew what they thought of her strange magic but had given up rationalizing her healing powers to others years ago. Quickly, she disappeared into the house to work on her patient.

She sat next to the girl and rubbed a dab of salve on her left knee. Then she gently released her spiders just below the potion. A hundred small creatures began to inject their venom into the girl, who immediately went limp. Estrilda rubbed a small amount of the attraction potion into the spider jar, and the spiders scurried back to their home. She repeated the process on the right knee. After the treatment, she put both jars on the floor by the child's bed.

Estrilda covered her eyes and chanted an incantation under her breath.

Velut luna
Statu variabilis
Semper crescis
Aut decrescis
Vita detestabilis
Vana salus
Semper dissolubilis
Obumbrata
Et velata

Estrilda turned to the parents.

"Will she be all right?" the mother asked.

"We will see," the healer said, reassuringly. "But all we can do now is wait."

Savaric led his wife to their little girl, who slept peacefully. He held his wife. Everything would soon be back to normal. He trusted Estrilda when his wife was in childbirth. Now, he trusted her with his daughter. She was a caring person even though she didn't look it. If she cured the girl, he would be forever in her debt.

~ 22 ~

Tolerance of strangers was never a virtue for the peasants of Valpechi. Thoughts of evil wizards or witches clouded their minds. Unseen enemies could wait a lifetime for their evil plots to come to fruition. The villagers needed to keep a constant vigil against the unknown in their midst. Witches casting spells on children could never result in a happy ending.

Shortly after Estrilda left the village with her small purse filled with coins, the villagers confronted Savaric outside his house.

"Why would you bring that woman into your home?"

"Can't you see, she brings evil into the whole village?"

"What are you talking about? She is a healer," Savaric shouted at the angry crowd.

They did not hear his words of reason. They were blinded by their superstitions and hatred of strangers.

"She is a witch," one of them cried.

"Maybe she was the one who killed the poor man in the woods!" screamed another.

"She travels from village to village. Who knows how many others she has murdered?" a third added.

Isn't it interesting to see how an angry crowd could solve the world's problems? A man is killed, and a stranger passes through your village a month later. The two events must be connected! All but the most dim-witted could see that the devil was at work here.

"Who knows, maybe your daughter is next!" shrieked another.

A scream came from inside Savaric's home as if to punctuate this ridiculous accusation. He ran through the door and was met by his wife. The little girl was shaking violently and hissing words that seemed to come from the devil himself.

"Seer alizo liet lavan juder leeher naast!"

The girl fell silent as if in a sleep of death. The villagers, who were uninvited, followed Savaric into his home and gasped in horror.

"The witch cast a spell on her."

"An evil spirit possesses her!"

The young girl's parents were too afraid to contradict the mob. They were terrified that their daughter might be possessed. In truth, she was only experiencing an extreme but harmless reaction to her humours flowing normally again in her body. The parents began to believe the dangerous tales their neighbors were spinning.

"We need to stop her before she kills again!"

The mob ran off, leaving the despondent parents to pray for their bewitched child. They caught Estrilda less than a mile down the deserted road as the sun was setting. Her old horse never moved very fast, and soon, the men from the village blocked her path, surrounding her with torches and plow shears turned into weapons.

"What do you want?" the old woman demanded.

"You have bewitched little Jamie and will pay for your evil deeds."

"What are you talking about, you ponce?"

"She spoke in tongues. She summoned the devil!"

"She was having a reaction to the venom but will be fine in the morning. I have seen it a hundred times."

"Did you hear? She said she cast hundreds of enchantments!"

"Take her!"

Estrilda raised a stick that she kept by her side for protection.

"Watch out! She's got her wand!"

The men were on the old woman before she could strike them. They dragged her off the wagon and threw her to the ground, tossing the stick into the field beside the road. The mob rocked the wagon back and forth until it rolled over. Estrilda screamed at the loss of her dearest possession. They set the wagon on fire. All manner of creatures escaped their cages and ran through the crowd, biting and cawing as they fled.

"A curse on your houses for your ignorance," the old woman bellowed.

She stood up to try to escape, but the men grabbed her.

"You'll be damned for this!" a villager screamed.

"Hold her tight. Witches can change shapes!"

None of the villagers had ever seen a witch do that. No one had ever seen a witch. Ignorant people make up facts to prove their warped reality. And these ill-bred farmers wanted to harm the woman because she was different.

"You are the ones who will be damned to hell for eternity," Estrilda cried.

She spit at the man standing in front of her. He replied by striking her with his fist. When she looked at him with defiance, he hit her again until she fell to the ground. The others joined in, beating her until she was unconscious. They studied the crumpled woman by the light of her burning wagon, breathing heavily, their anger barely satiated.

"What should we do with the witch? Should we finish this?"

"Witchcraft is a complicated problem."

"Kill her. That will end the problem!"

"She could rise again!"

"Not if we cut her in pieces!"

"If we dismember her, each piece could become another witch."

"S'truth!"

"Let's take her to the bishop in the capital. He will know how to destroy this unholy creature. Tie her up and make sure she can't escape."

With that, the villagers left their fields and families and made their way to the capital.

~ 23 ~

The royal carriage rolled through the streets of Aristal. Valdman had accompanied Prince John and Princess Ella on their return, riding in a second carriage. Although he felt ill at ease riding in a carriage, the king's ambassador needed a certain amount of prestige. The last time he was here, he and David were fugitives. Now, he held the future of the two kingdoms in his hands and was uncomfortable with that as well. The one thing he looked forward to was visiting the royal gardens. Valdman worked there when David was in the kitchen.

Those were happy times for the pair. Valdman knew they would be safe from King Peter's grasp working in his enemy's castle. David would practice his healing skills in the kitchen, cooking broths that contained magic herbs. The staff told David their worries, and he would nod slowly and add a bit of this and a dash of that. After the "patient" enjoyed a nice warm broth over a quiet conversation, they would go away happier and feeling better.

The head chef taught David all his tricks, and the student eagerly devoured the new knowledge. David took on more responsibility, and it wasn't long before he was running the kitchen. The chef would walk around clapping his hands and giving orders, but the staff knew who was in charge.

Valdman, for his part, tended a wild section at the far end of the garden. The place used to be a playground for the princes before he came to the castle, but it had been deserted for several years. He tended to the trees and the creatures within those forgotten woods. It reminded him of his life after his wife died, when he turned his back on society, went off into the dark forest of Dandorum, and became the wildman hunted by King Peter. The only difference was that he did not kill any intruders here. No poachers were trying to destroy this forest. These were protected woods, and he was rewarded for keeping them safe.

The carriages abruptly halted, shaking Valdman from his daydreams. He looked out the window. A group of ruffians dragged an old woman through the streets. A rowdy mob followed the scene, shouting and laughing. Valdman got out and asked a woman in the crowd.

"What is going on here?"

"They caught a witch," said the woman, with delight in her eyes.

"A witch? What will they do to her?"

"They are taking her to the bishop, where she will get what she deserves."

"What does she deserve?" Valdman questioned.

"To be sent back to the devil!"

"What did she do to deserve this fate?"

The woman thought for a moment. She did not know what crimes were committed but looked forward to the witch's execution regardless. She waved her hand to dismiss Valdman's concerns and rejoined the crowd.

Valdman walked to Prince John's carriage and tapped on their door. Cinderella opened it. Valdman climbed in.

"What is going on?" the prince said impatiently. "I must return to the castle to learn what urgent business called us home."

"Some people have found a witch and are bringing her to the bishop to be executed."

"A witch," Cinderella worried.

The prince looked at his wife and, sensing her concern, asked, "What is going on here?"

"If you wouldn't mind, Your Highness, I'd like to see what happens with the bishop. Do I have your permission to put our business on hold until I discover the truth?"

Cinderella looked at John. She feared for her daughter's safety again. Maybe an ally of Pesta had come to finish her plan! John knew a witch could not be caught that easily, but he wanted to comfort his wife. He smiled at her. She returned his smile.

"Please, ambassador, see what action the bishop takes and report back to us as soon as possible," John requested.

"Of course. I will present myself before the king shortly."

He nodded and left the carriage, following the excited crowd to the cathedral. He never knew the capital to be so frantic. People were running and yelling to their neighbors to join the crowd. He asked an anemic fellow why he was so anxious about a witch. The man looked at Valdman with disbelief and told him of the murders in the capital and outlying villages. The crowd wanted blood for blood.

"But what proof do you have that this person is a witch or that she did those things?"

A circle opened around him. The mob looked at him with suspicion. He recognized that look. They looked at him in the same way when he was caged in King Peter's square. He recognized the hatred of the unknown. Strangers were dangerous at this time.

"Prince John has just returned and asked me to find out what is happening."

That seemed to appease the crowd because they all walked away. Valdman followed them and soon entered the great plaza before the cathedral, which seemed more like a celebratory space than a place of quiet reflection. People sold fruits and vegetables to be eaten or thrown at the witch while she burned. The execution was not enough; public humiliation was also required. Children played tag, running between adults as they maneuvered to find the best viewing area. People searched for their friends. Pickpockets roamed through the crowd, looking for a purse dangling unprotected. Fights broke out. Priests from the cathedral called for calm, assuring the crowd that God's will would be done. Soldiers from the castle and constables from the cathedral patrolled the area.

Directly in front of Valdman, at the foot of the cathedral's steps, was an open circle where the poor woman lay prostrate on the ground. Father Jacob, a stout man living well off the donations of the poor, stood at the top of the steps and spoke to the crowd.

"But what proof do you have that she is a witch?" he asked, not seeming to care about the answer.

"She killed a child in our village," Malack, one of the men from Valpechi, cried out.

"Murder is a sin, but that does not make her a witch."

"The child was possessed by an evil spirit before she died. She called out to the Devil in a tongue no one could understand."

"That certainly would confirm your conclusion."

Valdman's eyes followed the building's spires up to the heavens. The spires represented knowledge, humility, and right actions. What behavior in this square reflected any of those ideals? Hatred and fear were the only emotions visible here. He silently vowed that he would not allow this woman to be killed for the entertainment of these ignorant people. He entered the circle.

"I am Valdman. Prince John sent me to investigate this matter."

"Welcome, Valdman from the castle. We are truly blest that our temporal leaders are concerned for our spiritual well-being," the priest proclaimed.

Valdman bowed ceremoniously to the priest and motioned for him to continue.

"Bain has been plagued since the prince's departure with an evil that has come right to these very steps. A poor potter was killed and left right here. Many soldiers also died defending our homes from the beast. Now it seems we have the creature that has done this evil."

"Priest, why does it seem that?"

"What?"

"Why does it seem that? This woman seems highly unlikely to be able to overpower a potter, to say nothing of trained soldiers."

"What are you saying?"

"Who are these people that have brought this woman here? Maybe they have some sort of grudge against her. If you are to execute God's judgment, shouldn't we have more than hearsay? What does the woman say in her defense?"

The priest looked at the unconscious woman.

"She doesn't seem willing to defend herself in this holy place before the eyes of God."

The crowd laughed. They did not want justice. They wanted blood.

Valdman interrupted their laughter, "Prince John and Princess Ella love their people. They want all of us to be safe, not just those who live inside the castle walls or the sanctuary of the church, but everyone."

The crowd softened its tone at the mention of Cinderella. Even after all these years, the poor girl elevated to royal status meant something to them.

Sensing an opening, Valdman continued, "What would Princess Ella do to this woman? Would she be so quick to condemn?"

"I don't believe that the princess is knowledgeable on the laws concerning witchcraft," the priest corrected the stranger, trying to regain his control.

Valdman knew he could not win that point, so he changed tactics.

"You may be right, but witches are crafty. If you do not destroy this evil completely, it will find another way to torment this city," Valdman conceded, seeming to agree with the priest.

"We will burn her like they did in Polsay," someone shouted from the crowd.

The crowd cheered, "Burn her, burn her."

Crowds are so easily led with angry words.

"What kind of witch is she? Is she a solitary witch? You might get rid of the problem with burning, but only if you could melt metal. If the fire is not hot enough, her gas will go into another person. Do you want her gas?" Valdman said, warning the crowd.

Valdman had no knowledge of melting witch temperatures or gases. He needed to buy the woman more time so calmer heads could prevail.

It seemed that the crowd did not want this witch's gas in them. They looked to their neighbors, hoping for reassurance, but only found confusion.

"And what if she is not a solitary witch? Where is her coven? Were there other creatures around when you captured the witch?" he asked the crowd.

"All sorts of creatures escaped from her wagon when we burned it!" one of the men who brought her to the cathedral said. His partners nodded in agreement.

"And you didn't capture them as well?" Valdman shook his head gravely.

"We'll burn her, then we'll deal with her coven," the priest shouted, feeling his hold on the crowd wane.

The rabble had grown quieter, no longer sure of what to feel.

"I know of the Polsay witch, and three weeks after they burned her, three goats and a chicken died mysteriously," Valdman continued his nonsensical arguments.

The people cried out in despair. What could they do to prevent such terrible events from happening here?

"What will you have us do?" The priest asked, exasperated.

"Take this woman to the bishop. He will surely have knowledge of the *Book of Domesday*, which will give us the correct answer."

Everyone looked to the priest, who flung his hands in the air and walked into the cathedral. The church constables lifted the unconscious woman and followed the priest. Valdman followed the constables until the guards at the entrance blocked his way.

The guards looked at him suspiciously. He demanded an audience with the bishop.

"Prince John commanded me to investigate this matter. To this end, I request an audience with the bishop as he contemplates the fate of the witch."

A constable went inside to receive instructions. Valdman looked at the remaining guards condescendingly. He turned his gaze to the crowd, which was growing larger by the moment. Soon, the guard returned and nodded to Valdman.

"Follow me, please," he said, walking through the vaulted doors.

Valdman silently followed.

~ 24 ~

Valdman followed the guard through the cathedral. Parishioners huddled in small groups, gossiping between prayers. They looked at Valdman with suspicion as he walked to the chapter house. Few people ever had business in the bishop's private residences, and they were curious about this stranger. They chattered like pigeons after the door closed behind him.

The guard stopped in front of the consistory court where matters of the church were decided far from public scrutiny. Valdman entered alone. It was just past midday, but the dark and somber room was lit primarily by candles. Scant natural light made it through the stained-glass windows darkened with the dirt of the city. In the shadows, at the far end of the room, was a large, raised chair whose back, barely silhouetted by the opaque windows, resembled the cathedral's three spires. Bishop Penk sat in the chair, his face shrouded in darkness. A large table surrounded by a three-foot wooden wall stood before the bishop. Eight priests sat at the table. Twenty cathedral constables protected the holy men from the witch who lay on the floor outside the enclosure. All heads, except for the unconscious witch, turned to Valdman. The bishop leaned into the light from his perch, revealing himself to the stranger.

"Please approach the bench," the bishop said kindly.

"Your Most Reverend Excellency," Valdman said, bowing as he approached. Hopefully, the holy man would stop this nonsense.

The bishop smiled. "Tell me, my son, what is your name?"

"William Valdman, your Excellency."

"Are you a member of the court? I don't recall meeting any William Valdman on my visits there."

"I am not from King Edward's court but from King David's. I accompanied Prince John here to negotiate a lasting peace between the kingdoms. Prince John asked me to discover the cause of the unrest in town."

"Negotiating peace is God's work," the bishop said thoughtfully.

"Thank you, your Excellency."

"I am concerned, William, that you feel the need to interfere with the church's business."

"I beg your pardon."

"What is Dandorum's business with this witch? Were you charged with this mission as well by your king?"

"No, your Excellency."

"Then why interfere? If the citizens want to burn a witch, let them burn a witch."

"But what if she isn't a witch?" Valdman countered.

"Well, what if she isn't?"

Valdman was stunned by the holy man's response.

"Then she is innocent," he stammered.

"Perhaps."

"Perhaps?" Valdman said, feeling his anger boiling inside.

"Who can say this is not God's will? Let him who is innocent throw the first stone and all that. She is probably guilty of a hundred crimes, each deserving death. God works in mysterious ways by giving us this sinner."

Valdman looked at the woman on the floor. She was just beginning to regain consciousness, unaware of the firestorm she was engulfed in. He looked at the priests sitting around the table. They seemed to be writing in slow motion, hardly aware that there was anyone else in the room. He shook his head.

All he could think to ask the bishop was, "But why?"

"Why what, my son?"

"Why allow me to speak on behalf of this woman if you had no intention to show her mercy?"

"I was curious about the man who spoke of The Domesday Book. When dealing with witches, I prefer The Malleus Maleficarum. The Domesday Book has nothing to do with the fate of witches."

"I am aware of that. I thought you would show her mercy."

"Her sentence hasn't changed, just the path to get there. You made this woman's journey a little longer. I believe our business has concluded."

Valdman took a deep breath before bowing to the bishop. "Your Excellency, I will share your decision with the prince."

Bishop Penk leaned back and dissolved into the darkness. Valdman turned to leave, but the bishop called him back.

"William," the bishop paused, waiting for Valdman to turn around. "I hope your negotiation skills are better than those you have demonstrated here."

"Yes, your Excellency."

Valdman walked from the room to sounds of subdued laughter from the priests sitting around the table. Bishop Penk's eyes narrowed as the intruder left his inner sanctum. This ambassadore could be dangerous and needed to be watched carefully.

"Take the witch to the crypt while we await word from the castle."

~ 25 ~

Valdman walked slowly to the castle. He dreaded telling the prince and Cinderella that an innocent person would be executed as a witch. David taught him to be forgiving of people. *Weakness and meanness exist in all of us, and we must accept the bad with the good.* Valdman felt the call of the wildman urging him to destroy the bigoted, small-minded people who delighted in the death of the innocent old woman.

But the walk through the small winding streets away from the cathedral cleared his mind. The quiet streets sported no crowds anxiously awaiting a public murder, shouting for blood in the afternoon sun. Someone played a violin on the upper floor of a three-story building on Trinity Lane. The sound bounced against the stone facades, making it impossible to tell where the music came from. Two children played in the street outside a bakery. They tossed several stones and then danced an intricate pattern around them, giggling with every step. Valdman smiled at them as he walked by, remembering what he had long ago forgotten.

He passed the shops of a carpenter and a surgeon. His tongue rubbed a tender back tooth, but he had no time to get it looked at today. These modern surgeons could produce miracles. Imagine being able to extract a tooth, relieving years of pain! But despite all the medical advancements, people remained angry and petty.

As he entered the castle gates, his thoughts returned to the woman. The throne room was filled with courtiers and servants when he presented himself to the king.

Meetings in the throne room are all pomp and circumstance, bluster with no substance. Generally, the monarch both welcomes and humbles the visitor to remind him before whom he stands, as if there were any question. The visitor will be humiliated unless he possesses some secret weapon to even the score. A wise man will keep his cards hidden and not give anything away. Nothing of substance happens here, just a show of power.

"Welcome, ambassador of Dandorum," King Edward bowed his head slightly.

"Dandorum thanks Your Highness, for extending the invitation to continue peace talks. King David hopes Your Highness is in good health now that your wartime physician has returned to rule his country." Valdman returned the bow.

"Yes, I am in good health, but I miss David's remedies on the battlefield and his creations in my kitchen," Edward smiled, acknowledging the shared history. "You were with him while he was in Bain, I recall?"

"Yes, Your Majesty. I worked in your gardens while King David worked in your kitchens."

"How many spies from Dandorum worked in my castle?" the king smiled.

"Your Majesty, I am not aware of any spies," Valdman returned the smile but knew that King Edward was a man not to be trusted. He was a shrewd ruler, and Valdman needed to be cautious.

"Valdman, there are always spies; if you were not one, there were others. Have you settled into your rooms yet?"

"No, Your Majesty, Prince John asked me to look into a matter in the city. I have just arrived."

"My son has informed me of the matter. Please, settle in from your long journey."

"Thank you, Your Highness, but I am anxious to continue negotiations so our kingdoms can exist in peace."

"Prince John will not continue negotiations. He has other matters to attend to now that he has returned. This is Samuel Bamberger. He will handle discussions from our side," the king said offhandedly.

Bamberger stepped forward from behind the king and bowed to Valdman. His bearing spoke of years of military service.

Valdman was surprised but not shaken by this tactic. Changing negotiators usually means you are not satisfied with how things are going. Talks had hardly begun, so where could there be dissatisfaction? Valdman wondered if there were more pressing issues than peace between the two kingdoms.

"Very well, Your Highness," Valdman said, retiring to his rooms.

~ 26 ~

Valdman waited in the grand solar on the castle's third floor to meet Prince John and Princess Ella. The large windows let in enough light to warm the room in the winter. The rich tapestries on the walls depicted pastoral scenes. In contrast, the tapestries in the throne room illustrated great battles in which Bain was victorious. The difference in decorations stated that this room was for secretive meetings, not public ceremonies, so things could be accomplished here. A servant came in and brought Valdman a cup of warm mulled wine. He closed his eyes to calm his mind in this quiet, peaceful place.

"We weren't so long, Ambassador, to put you asleep?" Cinderella said, smiling.

Prince John followed her into the room.

Valdman stood and bowed, "No, Your Highness, I was appreciating a moment of solitude before our meeting."

"Was the wine to your liking?" The prince asked.

"Yes, Your Highness. When I was here, I always enjoyed the excesses of your vineyards."

"I didn't know there was such a thing as an excess of wine," the prince smiled.

John indicated to Valdman to take a seat, leading him to a small circle of carved wooden chairs. Cinderella and the two men sat down and talked in hushed tones.

"William, what about the woman by the cathedral?" Cinderella asked, cutting the frivolity of the moment.

"I am sorry, but I have no good news to report. The woman dealt with potions, and it seemed she might have hurt a young girl. The villagers have accused her of being a witch."

"Did she purposefully hurt the girl?"

"I do not believe she did, Princess."

"But surely the bishop does not believe such silliness," the prince said sharply.

"The bishop believes it is better to let her die than to take the chance that she is a witch and let her go."

The three sat in silence. Finally, Cinderella asked.

"William, do you think she is a witch?"

He studied the royals for a moment.

"No, Your Highness, I have met a witch, and this woman is not one."

"A witch?" Cinderella recoiled.

John instinctively went to protect his wife, taking her hand.

"Yes, long ago, my wife was ill, and I went to a witch to see if she had a potion to help. She gave me the means to save my wife."

"Did she recover?" the Princess asked, hopefully.

"No, Your Highness, by the time I returned, my family was murdered, and my village was destroyed."

"By whom?" the prince demanded.

"By King Peter, during the first war with your father," he looked at the prince.

"But didn't you live in Dandorum?" asked John, confused.

"That is correct, but the king wanted to show what would happen for disloyalty."

"Were they disloyal?" The prince questioned Valdman, trying to find some justification for this terrible act.

"No, Your Majesty. Some rulers like to make big statements. Justice is not always a priority."

"Not all rulers are unjust. King Edward is not like Peter," corrected the prince quietly.

Prince John remembered what Pesta told him about his father. People can justify the worst crimes to achieve their goals.

Valdman looked at them. "Your father was about to execute David, though he knew the charges against him were false."

Prince John looked down. The Princess looked at her husband.

"But he can't let that mob kill an innocent woman," she said, standing.

"Where are you going?" John asked.

"I am going to see the king."

"You can't," he said, following her to the door.

"And why not?" she demanded.

"Because," John hesitated. "that is church business. My father will not interfere with the decisions of the bishop."

"He must do something, John." Tears filled her eyes. "There must be some kindness in people. Ruling cannot be only about enforcing judgment against the weak and helpless. There must be some compassion still left in this world, some mercy."

"I'm afraid the matter is out of our hands. May her soul find peace," the prince said, trying to make his wife understand the ways of the court.

Cinderella turned from her husband. How could she accept disguising cruelty for the rule of law? How could she accept injustice where justice and mercy should prevail? She left the room angrily.

Valdman and the prince looked at each other before turning away. They understood the injustice of the situation. Cinderella forced them to examine their own dishonesty.

Valdman was embarrassed that this was the circle in which he now traveled. Living was much simpler in the deep, dark forest where every act was justified for survival. Here, the world moved with a different rhythm. Rules have more power than righteousness. Pomp is more important than kindness.

The prince thought of his guilt. The time spent on his quest to bring Anne home taught him empathy for his subjects. Was he not responsible for the woman's death if he did nothing to prevent it? Was he as cruel as his father was to the witch Pesta? Was he as murderous as Peter? Does acceptance of a brutal act make you complicit? John knew he continued to be part of an evil system.

"Thank you for your efforts on behalf of the woman," the prince said after another moment.

"We are not responsible for the cruelty of institutions we find ourselves in," Valdman said, sensing the prince's sadness.

"I can't help but think we are, William," John said as he left.

Valdman sat at the table and cradled the warm cup in his hands. Bits of clove and cinnamon floated in his wine, islands in a crimson sea. He thought of his wife, whom he had lost a lifetime ago.

~ 27 ~

"I am sorry, Princess Ella, there is nothing to be done," the king said.

The throne room was filled, and the king was not happy with Cinderella disturbing his business with this nonsense.

"But you must help the poor woman!" she said forcefully.

The king would not be challenged in his court.

"Why? Why *must* I help her?"

"Because she is innocent!"

"How do you know this? Have you questioned her?"

"No, I haven't, Your Highness."

"Then why do you presume this witch is innocent?"

"I believe-"

"So, we are to rule our country on your beliefs? Do you have any knowledge of sorcery?"

"No, Sire."

" You want me to interfere with church business and jeopardize our entire way of life because you believe something about someone you have never spoken to! The church and state must not impose their will on the other. Each is separate. Each is distinct. They are in a delicate balance well beyond your understanding, girl."

"Have mercy!"

"Mercy! Please! That is just an excuse for avoiding justice. Did your husband send you here?"

"No, Your Majesty."

"Well, I suggest you hurry back to him where you belong and not bother the court again. The next time you disturb the king's business, I will not be so lenient."

The crowded room was silent. Cinderella felt like the whole world was watching her, delighting in her humiliation. She bowed deeply.

"Yes, Your Majesty," she said, turning quickly.

Before she took three steps, King Edward stopped her.

"A moment, Princess."

Cinderella turned back to him.

"Yes, Your Majesty?"

The king whispered something to Bamberger, who nodded. The king turned back to the Princess but immediately returned to his advisor. Cinderella wondered if the conversation was about her. The eyes of the court focused on her. The third time the king whispered to Bamberger, it became clear that the king wanted to extend her humiliation. She could not leave until he excused her, but she could not speak until she was acknowledged. Cinderella was caught in a temporal purgatory created by the king, and her punishment would be eternal. The king finally smiled at her.

"Oh, nothing. You are dismissed."

~ 28 ~

That night, Cinderella had trouble sleeping. She used to wander the castle at night, hoping to find meaning. That was when she became friends with David, the kitchen boy and future king. She found herself back in the kitchen.

The room felt empty without him, with only the embers in the hearth casting a slight orange glow. When her eyes became accustomed to the darkness, she felt an uneasiness envelope her. Then she saw a figure sitting at the table with his back to her.

She gasped. The figure stood up, turning towards her. It was Valdman.

"I'm sorry to startle you, Princess," he said, bowing.

"What are you doing here?" she uttered.

Valdman lit a twig near the fireplace. He then used the fire to light a lamp on the table, and the light brightened the room.

"I could not sleep and came here for a cup of tea. I'm sorry to have frightened you."

"Please sit down. I am sorry to disturb you. I was unable to sleep with all the trouble in the city."

"Would you like some tea, Princess? It will help you sleep," Valdman offered.

The Princess smiled but turned to go. After a few steps, she stopped and turned to him.

"Please."

She cautiously approached the table and sat across from where he was standing. Valdman brought a cup for the Princess and placed it before her. She smiled but avoided making eye contact.

He went around the table and picked up the cast-iron teapot. He returned to her side of the table and filled her cup. He returned to his side and waited. She looked at him for a moment before realizing he wanted her permission to sit.

"Please," she said.

"Thank you," he took his seat.

They sat in silence, staring into their cups of tea. He took a sip, trying not to slurp. He remembered being the wildman in a cage in Dandorum. Now, he was sitting having tea with a princess. He never thought he would live that long.

She took a sip, used to not slurping from years of scrutiny in this dismal castle. The tea burned her lips.

"Hot," she sputtered.

He smiled, "Yes, sorry."

She returned his smile before both fell into silence again.

After a few more moments, Cinderella offered, "It has been a long time since I have found myself in this kitchen at night."

"Yes," he said.

They thought of David. After a few more moments.

"How is your king?"

"David?"

"Yes."

"He is the king."

"Yes."

"Many decisions to ponder. Many questions to rule on."

"Yes."

"At times, I am sure he misses a simpler life."

"Being a kitchen boy?"

"Yes."

"Sometimes I miss the simpler life as well. I'm sure your current position can be uncomfortable at times."

As if to answer her, Valdman stood. Cinderella turned to the door. Prince John was standing in the shadows. She stood.

Prince John broke the silence. "I was wondering where you were, Ella."

"I was having trouble sleeping. I thought a cup of tea would help me. Ambassador Valdman was enjoying a pot when I entered. He offered me a cup, and I joined him."

John entered the room and walked to his wife. He took the cup from the table and had a sip.

"What is in this tea?"

"Agrimony for healing. Lavander for rest. Bergalilly for sweetness and keeping evil away."

"Evil?" the prince inquired suspiciously.

"There is always evil. In addition, it tastes good," Valdman replied.

"Yes, it does," the prince said, finishing the cup. "Are you ready, Ella?"

She nodded, and they walked to the door. When the prince reached the entrance, he turned to the ambassador.

"Because of the history of this room and visitors from Dandorum, I recommend all future tea parties take place in the daylight with servants present. Do you agree?"

"I am here to negotiate a lasting peace with your kingdom. That is my only priority, Your Highness," Valdman pledged, bowing to the prince.

"Very well then," the prince said as he left the room.

~ 29 ~

The cathedral guards dragged Estrilda down to the crypt, where she would be beaten until she confessed. This would not take long as her torturers were well practiced in extracting the truth from sinners.

She was still groggy as they put her on the rack, but the woman recovered her senses when bone separated from cartilage. She begged for mercy.

Captain Umfrey, the torturer-in-chief, and his two helpers were not accustomed to giving mercy, especially to those accused of witchcraft. They believed in what they were doing, ridding the world of Satan's evil. They had wives and children they loved and wanted to protect from this sinful world. These good men did not see the woman lying on the rack as a person. They saw her as a servant of the Devil. They turned the cranks further, and her bones popped as they left their sockets.

"Please, please, I beg you," she pleaded.

The men continued despite her cries and did not stop until the bishop appeared at the door. He was always kind to these men. Bishop Penk appreciated his servants who carried out terrible deeds in Jesus' name. Not many people would have the stomach for this job. You cannot be squeamish in the service of God.

"Has she confessed?" the bishop softly asked the captain.

"No, your Excellency, but it shouldn't be too long."

"Good. We want to conclude this business quickly to show our parishioners that the loving arms of the church protect them."

"Please, please, I beg you," the woman moaned softer than the last time.

The bishop walked to the woman and studied his guest. He touched her arm gently, but she screamed in pain. He quickly removed his hand and looked at the captain, approving the torturer's admirable work.

"What is it, my child?" He looked at her with compassion.

"Mercy, please."

"God gives mercy. All you have to do is accept it."

"How can I do that?"

"You have to confess."

"What have I done?"

"You are a witch."

"A witch?"

"Yes, a witch. You were apprehended while practicing your dark arts in Valpechi. You bewitched a young girl."

"No, your Excellency, I helped the child."

Bishop Penk looked at the captain and his men. They turned the wheel another notch. The woman screamed.

"Please, please!"

"Are you a witch?" the bishop asked kindly.

Estrilda looked into his eyes. She knew that a man with such kind eyes would surely be merciful.

"Yes, your Excellency," she whimpered as tears rolled down her cheeks.

"Very good, my child. You have been bad, haven't you?"

"Yes, I have been bad."

"You bewitched that girl, haven't you?"

"I did."

"And you have caused the trouble in our city."

"I have not been to Aristal in several months."

The bishop looked to his men. They turned the notch again.

The woman cried, "Yes, I have. Please, please."

Estrilda was hardly coherent through her pain. The bishop continued passively.

"But how did such a frail woman as yourself kill all those men, even castle guards? That hardly seems possible. Unless..." his eyes flashed with inspiration. "Captain, can you send one of your men to ask the villagers who brought her here if this witch had a belt with her?"

"A belt?"

"Yes, an ornate belt with strange symbols on it?"

The captain signaled one of his men to complete the task. The captain looked puzzled.

The bishop explained, "There is the tale of the werewolf of Bedburg. The Devil himself had given a villager a magical belt, which enabled him to change into a greedy, devouring wolf, strong and mighty, with eyes great and large, which in the night sparkled like fire, a mouth with sharp and cruel teeth, a huge body, and mighty paws. Removing the belt made him transform back to his human form. This witch has the power of transformation. She is the beast that has terrified the capital. Her death will end this evil."

The captain and his men looked terrified. As cruel as the torturers were, they could not compete with the Prince of Darkness. Bishop Penk could see through deception to the truth. No matter how she pleaded, this woman was a servant of the Devil, and no mercy could be shown.

That moment, in the dark and foul-smelling room, was momentous. The bishop sensed the power he held and felt joyful. He took a slow breath in. God is good and shows himself in the direst of circumstances. The room was silent except for the soft groans of the old woman and the pitter-patter of a stray rat as it scurried in the darkest corners of the room, looking for a piece of flesh. The serenity was delicious. Penk's happiness was short-lived, however, as the constable returned.

"'I'm sorry, Reverend, the villagers saw no belt."

"Pity, that would have simplified things. No matter, the old ways are the best. You may continue your interrogation, captain. Don't take too long; people want to feel safe in their homes."

"Yes, your Excellency."

"Oh, captain, it might be best if you break her legs so she can't escape either before or after death."

"Yes, your Excellency."

"Good," the bishop smiled. "I look forward to the conclusion of this business."

The bishop left. He had no stomach for what would come next. The captain watched the holy man leave before picking up his axe. He raised it slowly above his head and brought the blunt end down on the woman's shins. She would not be walking anywhere today.

~ 30 ~

"What are you doing in my garden?" Princess Anne demanded.

She had not seen Valdman before and was suspicious of strangers.

"Pardon me, Princess," he apologized, rising from picking bergalilly flowers. "My name is William Valdman. I am an ambassador from Dandorum and have come to negotiate peace between our two kingdoms."

"What do I care why you are here? Does that permit you to steal from my garden?"

She approached him aggressively. He stepped back and bowed to the royal. He remembered that he would have bellowed and frightened off this spoiled little princess not too long ago. But now, he had to be polite. He bit his cheek and remained silent.

She grabbed his sachet, where he kept the bits of bark, twigs, and flowers he had collected. She opened it and spilled the contents on the ground.

"No, Princess-" he contained his anger and started again. "I was collecting some twigs to make a soothing tea."

"Are you some kind of witch? There are witches around, you know. They just caught one in town!" she proclaimed.

"I am not a witch. I am a healer. And you should not worry. The woman in town is not a witch either."

"How do you know? Have you ever met a real witch?"

"Yes, Princess, I have. Her name was Pesta."

Anne's eyes widened. She looked around to see that no one was looking. She approached Valdman as he collected the herbs on the ground.

"I don't believe you! What sort of trick is this?" she growled.

"This is no trick, I promise you. This is agrimony for healing. This is lavander for rest. I use bergalilly to sweeten the tea. Spider Wood will keep away evil."

He held the last herb up, close to the princess. She stepped back and lost her balance. Abby, who was never far behind the princess, caught her mistress before she fell. Anne regained her equilibrium and slapped her dress as if there were dirt on it.

"You've got dirt on me, you horrible man. You will be punished for your impertinence."

"I am sorry for my impertinence. It won't happen again," he bowed again to the princess.

"I don't know anything about your stupid roots and berries. I will tell my father and mother about you, and you will pay!" she threatened.

She stormed off. Valdman looked at Anne as she left and then at the root in his hand.

"Very curious."

~ 31 ~

After several days of lying near death, Jamie opened her eyes and looked around. Her father was sleeping on the floor next to her, his head resting on her cot. Her mother was sweeping the dirt out the door of their one-room home. Jamie sat up in bed and smiled. She liked her parents being around her, as all young children do at her age.

"I'm hungry," she announced.

The woman dropped the broom and ran to her daughter.

"Savaric!" she cried joyfully.

Her husband lifted his head slowly, still in the grip of sleep. He looked up to see his wife embracing their daughter. Jamie smiled at her father.

"Hello, daddy. Mommy's squeezing too hard."

"Jamie!" He laughed and joined his wife, holding their daughter.

The family made a ball of hands, arms, and heads rocking, grasping, and laughing. Squeals of delight and giggles filled the small house as no one wanted to break the happiness. The stress of the last few days as their daughter lay close to death was too much for Emma, and she broke down. Jamie saw her mother's sorrow and began to cry as well.

"What is the matter, mother?"

"Nothing, my darling. We were worried about you."

The young girl looked to her father for reassurance, but he was also crying. Jamie could not understand her parents' emotions. She thought she was responsible for their pain.

Emma looked at her daughter and husband. They were sobbing, but she began to giggle. Why were they crying at such happiness? Jamie followed her mother. Their laughter made Savaric laugh, and so they all laughed.

This is how the family spent some time, between tears and laughter. Finally, one by one, they fell asleep from exhaustion in each other's arms.

Later that night, the family sat down to a meal of thanksgiving.

"Thank you, Lord, for restoring Jamie to health," Savaric prayed, looking at his daughter, who smiled shyly. "And thank you for sending Estrilda to us to fulfill your desire that all your servants should live in peace and comfort throughout their days. And, of course, thank you for my wonderful wife, the best cook, mother, and wife in the village."

"Just in the village?" Emma smiled at her husband.

"Did I say village? I meant the kingdom, of course."

"Of course," his wife said.

"Of course," mimicked little Jamie.

All this happiness ended after the girl had gone to bed.

"Estrilda has been taken to the capital for practicing witchcraft," Emma spoke softly so as not to wake their daughter.

"How do you know this?" Savaric gasped.

"Gundred said her husband and the other men caught her and took her to the bishop."

"Malack? He was always an ignorant one. Couldn't he see she was helping us?"

"People see what they want to see, Savaric. What can you do?" she shrugged.

"What could I do? I have to help her!"

"Don't be dim, husband. How can you help her? You are a poor farmer," her frustration with her husband began to show.

"I could go to the capital and explain that she is no witch."

"Who would listen to you?"

"Emma, everything that we have, we owe to Estrilda. Without her help during childbirth, you and Jamie might not have survived. She brought Jamie back to us today. How can we do nothing?"

"I don't know," Emma answered softly.

"I don't know either. I will leave first thing in the morning."

"Do you really think you could help?"

"I know I have to try."

"Then we will try as well."

"What are you saying, Emma?"

"If you go, we will go also."

"Jamie is too weak."

"She is strong enough. And who knows? When Malack sees that Jamie is cured, maybe he will tell the bishop that he made a mistake."

"They won't be able to deny the truth in front of their eyes." Savaric held his wife in his arms.

"And the journey to the capital will be a wonderful adventure." Emma smiled.

"For better or worse."

"It has only been good, even in the bad times."

They walked over to where Jamie was sleeping and held each other close.

"You are right, Emma. Even in the bad times, it has been good."

The diminishing embers from the hearth darkened the room in the quiet night. All was calm. All was right.

~ 32 ~

Cinderella sat in her room by the window overlooking the gardens. The world looked so beautiful, all green and peaceful. In the capital, the world was not at peace. Estrilda was to be executed soon, another victim of the fear gripping the city.

Cinderella thought of her trip with John. Being alone with him had done so much to renew their love. But what kind of chance has love got in a place like this? Between an evil creature roaming the streets at night, to the unholy holy men, to a monarch only concerned with appearances. Cinderella wondered if the world had always been this cruel or had only recently become so.

Her life had not been easy. She had suffered the loss of her mother and father when she was so young and the tyranny of her stepmother and sisters. Finally, finding her true love, only to realize it was a sham. Her daughter was abducted. The absence of her husband led to loneliness and isolation. And then depression.

There was one perfect moment at the ball when she first met her prince. That first dance. The moment when he took her in his arms. She had never felt so safe. Yes, that was the moment!

Are we only allowed one perfect moment in our lives? What happens then? Should we just be thankful to some higher power for his occasional generosity? For one moment of joy lost in a thousand dark events. Maybe it would be better not to have had that moment at all. Then, we would not have something good to compare the bad times to. We would not know how horrible our lives are.

"Hello, Mother. At your window again?" Princess Anne and Abby were standing by the door of her chambers.

"Hello, Anne," Cinderella smiled weakly, still thinking her dark thoughts.

"You spend so much time at your window. I believe you wish you were a little bird, able to fly from your castle prison to a far-away place."

"Where would I go?" she asked her daughter.

Princess Anne smiled, "I would go back to my home."

"But this is your home."

"I would go to my real home, Mother Pesta's castle."

Cinderella's heart sank. She turned away from her daughter and caught Abby's eyes momentarily before looking out the window. Abby was a strange creature. She had an air of impassivity about her, which seemed to hide understanding. Whatever secrets were hidden in the servant were likely to stay there.

A moment passed in silence. Then Cinderella summoned the courage to address her hurtful daughter. She stood to present a dignified exterior as she crumbled inside.

"Anne, most people have hopes for adventures in far-off places, but we must be thankful for where we are now. You were taken from me when you were so young. All those years I spent without you, but now you are home. You are home, and you will grow to love this place. I promise you. Just give it a little more time."

"Do you love this place, Mother, with its corruption and evil? Wouldn't you trade all of it for one moment under the big weeping willow tree playing 'Catch Me' with your mother and father?"

"We can't change our past. The present is all we can alter."

"What would you like to alter, Mother? There must be some-thing. This cannot be the life you want. We are both prisoners here."

"I would like it to be a little different. I think your father loves me and we could be happy. I would like for the little girl I knew to return. You were so kind and gentle. I hope you will give me a chance."

"I am not that girl. I could give you, my servant. She is stupid and quiet, and you can pretend that she loves you."

Anne walked to Abby and angrily took her arm, "Girl, do you love my mother? Do you? Do you, girl?"

Anne threw her to the ground. Cinderella sprang to Abby's rescue and lifted her. She hugged her, a substitute for her own flesh and blood.

"What has she done to you? What have I done to you, Anne? Whatever it is, please forgive me. I am sorry."

"Give her back to me," Anne said, pulling Abby away. "This place makes a person feeble, and she will need to be strong for what is to come. This place! Filled with manners and customs created to make people soft. Follow your king! Follow your God! Don't think! Don't act! Be weak and humble!"

"What are you saying?" Cinderella cried, afraid of her own daughter.

"I heard what the king did to you, how he humiliated you for his amusement. How many times has he humiliated you before? What did you do to deserve such treatment?"

"I asked for mercy."

"That is how the king responds to kindness, with anger. Whose mercy did you plead for?"

"A woman accused of being a witch."

"If she were a witch, she would need no mercy."

"I believe she is innocent."

Anne advanced on Cinderella.

"So, this is how the innocent are treated in your kingdom? Humiliated and executed? No wonder these rulers say you will be rewarded after death. Quite a trick, and you are a part of the illusion. They hold you up and say, *look what you can have if you are a good person. You can become a princess!*"

"I did not marry your father to live in a castle. I loved him."

"Loved?"

"Love. I love him."

Anne laughed. She looked out the window to the green gardens and forests beyond.

"I see why you like looking out this window. So peaceful. I like my view overlooking the town. Tomorrow, I will see smoke rising as religious men burn an innocent woman while the king and his subjects rejoice. A metaphor for life in this terrible place. And you called Pesta wicked!"

Anne smiled as Cinderella sank back in her chair. The younger Princess turned away and left the room. Abby looked at Cinderella for a moment before following.

~ 33 ~

The torturers hauled the witch to the cathedral square the following afternoon. She cried in pain from her injuries as her legs dragged uselessly behind her. They had been broken above and below the knees, and her arms dislocated from their sockets. She would not escape her punishment or the grave. Unholy creatures can expect no redemption, only darkness and suffering.

Father Jacob led the procession from the dungeons. Next came four church soldiers, followed by the chief torturer, who raised his axe to the delight of the crowd. His assistants completed the parade by dragging Estrilda behind them. The crowd parted as they solemnly passed. The priest stopped in front of the pyre and behind the chopping block. This was the stage for the final act of this drama. The crowd quieted as the priest prepared to speak.

"People of Aristal, here is the witch Estrilda. Her trial before Bishop Penk was fair and just, and the witch, confronted by His Holiness, could not conceal her numerous sins. She confessed freely to sorcery and more. She has confessed to witchcraft since the age of twelve. Livestock have died mysteriously after she had passed through the towns surrounding our capital. She has concubined with the Devil and his demons. Because of this, the Devil has given her the power to transform into a wild beast with flaming eyes, poisonous breath, and jagged teeth. She has murdered innocent people in our city."

As he spoke, the spectators cried out in fear. Mothers covered their children's ears. Women fainted, and the young men drifted further away from Father Jacob in case the creature would regain consciousness and attack. But the torturers did their job well. The poor woman would not see another day.

The priest continued, "The bishop consulted the holy books and church protocols to find the correct punishment for the crimes committed. He prayed to the Holy Father for guidance. After hours of quiet contemplation, the answer was revealed to him. The witch, having confessed her sins against God and man, shall be beheaded to set an example to others who choose the path of devilry. After her death, she shall be burned upon this pyre so her body will not rise from its unholy grave. Her head will be impaled on a post for you to throw stones at. The holy bishop has blessed the stones at the booth to the right so you can purchase them and show how sinners are treated."

The crowd cheered. They were tired of living in fear and surged forward, wanting to be closer to the event. The cathedral soldiers quickly entered the square, pushing back the crowd so they would not be splattered by unholy blood.

The torturers dragged Estrilda to the chopping block. They tied her neck to the block and stepped on her hands to prevent her from moving. The captain prided himself on a quick cut that cleanly separated the head from the body. Some other executioners did not mind a double chop or a hack, hack, hack to get the job done, but not him. Last night, he stayed up late sharpening his blade. He was ready and proud to execute God's judgment on Earth. He lifted his blade high above his head.

"Wait," a voice from the crowd cried.

Everyone turned to see who had spoken at such an inopportune moment. Father Jacob stopped praying for the witch's soul. The executioner looked to the father for guidance. The priest turned to find the person who had interrupted the solemn proceedings. It was Savaric and his family, who had only just arrived in the capital. The crowd parted to include the newcomers. Savaric at once felt small. He was a poor farmer, not used to attention.

"Who are you, sir? And why have you disrupted this holy ceremony?" Father Jacob demanded.

"My name is Savaric, Father. I come from Valpechi. This woman tended to my daughter, Jamie. This is my wife, Emma."

"Well, Savaric from Valpechi, why have you interrupted the execution of this witch?"

"She is no witch. She is a healer. My daughter is proof that she uses her knowledge for good."

"A witch can do good to cover larger evils. Witnesses have given testimony that the child spoke in tongues."

"She had a fever. She was unwell," the mother pleaded.

"And she is no longer ill?"

"No, father. Her fever has subsided." Savaric assured the priest.

Father Jacob motioned to the guards to grab the girl. As she was separated from her parents, she shrieked incomprehensibly. Emma yelled for the guards to stop. Other guards grabbed her before she could rescue her child. Savaric sprung at the soldiers but was beaten unconscious. The crowd gasped.

"She is possessed," someone cried.

The crowd backed away, afraid of what would happen next.

"They all are," shouted another faceless voice from the crowd.

"You are right," the priest yelled. "This family must also be servants of the Devil sent to defend a witch tried and convicted of sins beyond comprehension. These servants of the Devil are attacking us. Who will listen to them and turn away from God?"

People cried out to the Lord above. Why was such evil upon them?

The soldiers dragged the unconscious man to the cathedral steps and threw him down. Father Jacob motioned to the soldiers, who released the woman and the child. They ran to Savaric.

"What shall we do with these creatures of evil? Do we need a trial when their guilt is obvious?" the priest bellowed.

"No!" screamed the crowd in a wild frenzy.

"Who believes that God's justice is swift?"

"Aye!"

"Then he who is righteous, let him throw the first stone!"

The crowd ran to the stand with the rocks and used them to stone mother, father, and daughter on the steps of that holy cathedral. As their blood ran onto the square, the executioner picked up his axe and separated the witch's head from her body quite cleanly.

The witnesses cheered and cried out with tears of joy. They had banned evil from their city all at once. No longer would the Devil come to Aristal!

A young boy picked up the witch's head to scare his friends. Soldiers chased him until he dropped it. Happy bystanders kicked the head. Finally, the soldiers recovered it. They impaled it on a pole to jeers and laughter. The people were safe once again.

The crowd helped throw the witch and the family on the pyre. It was good that they built it large. It easily accommodated the four bodies because the youngest witch was quite small. The crowd cheered as the bodies were doused with oil and set aflame.

Princess Anne watched the smoke rise from the cathedral square. She could hear the distant cheers and merriment. Her eyes narrowed with hatred as the sun set over the city.

34

Prince John sat in his study, reading. He hadn't had time for books when he was on his quest but since his return, he indulged when he could.

Someone knocked on the door.

"Come in," the prince responded.

Valdman entered. The prince looked disappointed.

"Oh."

Valdman could read the displeasure on John's face.

"I beg your pardon, Your Majesty. Is this a bad time?"

"No, please come in."

The prince put down his book and beckoned Valdman to approach.

"I must inform you that I will no longer be discussing the peace between our two kingdoms," the prince said. "As of now, Bamberger will oversee negotiations on behalf of our kingdom."

"Pardon, Your Majesty, but I have come to talk with you and the princess on a completely different matter."

"Oh? Please sit down," the prince gestured to the empty chair beside him.

Valdman glanced at the book and smiled, "Ah, *Ars Amatoria*. Ovid."

The prince looked surprised, "Oh, you know of him?"

"Yes. The ends justify the deed," he said, quoting the poet.

"Let others praise ancient times; I am glad I was born in these," the prince countered.

They smiled at one another before remembering the reality of the times they lived in. They looked away, embarrassed.

"We could all use a little help, you know, in our most intimate moments," The prince shrugged, referring to Ovid.

"Yes, yes, of course," Valdman agreed. And after another pause, "Not really."

An uncomfortable silence followed.

"I wanted to thank you for the tea, William," the prince said. "I can't remember when I slept better."

"Thank you, Your Majesty, and again, I did not mean for the chance meeting with Princess Ella to give the impression of impropriety."

"I understand."

Neither of them noticed Cinderella standing in the doorway, smiling.

"Are you two friends now?" she asked.

The men turned towards her and shifted uncomfortably. The prince hid his book behind a pillow on the settee. Valdman stood and bowed awkwardly.

"I would like to thank you as well. I enjoyed the conversation *and* the tea," Cinderella smiled at the blushing boys.

Valdman recovered his composure. "I am glad you have joined us, Princess Ella. As I was just telling the prince, I have a matter that I wish to share with both of you."

His tone worried Cinderella. She sat next to her husband, feeling like a guilty child worried that she was about to be punished for some wrongdoing.

Valdman took out his pouch and removed the spider wood root, handing it to Cinderella. She studied it carefully before giving it to her husband.

"This is called spider wood or the Devil's Claw," Valdman explained.

The prince and princess stiffened at the mention of the name. The prince handed the root back to him.

Valdman continued, "The herb protects against evil and enchantments."

"Enchantments?" Cinderella faltered.

"If someone is under a spell, this can help the person escape it."

"What does this have to do with us?" the prince demanded.

"Please, let me explain. I was in the garden the other day collecting herbs for my teas. I met your daughter."

"Oh," the princess said, barely above a whisper.

"She demanded to know what was in my pouch. When I showed her this herb, she recoiled. I've never known that to happen unless..."

"Unless?" The prince challenged.

"Unless Anne was enchanted," Cinderella said quietly.

"Yes," Valdman responded just as quietly.

The parents looked at each other. They suspected this but had not had the courage to say it. It horrified them but also gave them hope. If Anne was enchanted, then there could be a remedy! Maybe, maybe, they would soon have their loving daughter back again! They turned to Valdman.

"What can we do?" Cinderella asked, determined.

"Princess, I don't know whether I am correct. It is only a suspicion I have. And it would help if I knew which spell she is under."

"Pesta was a powerful witch. Are you sure you could do something?" John asked.

"Pesta? I met her once, and it almost cost me my life," Valdman replied. "Each sorceress has her favorite spell. Hopefully, I can narrow it down. If I could talk with Anne and her servant separately, I might be able to figure it out."

"It would be difficult to do that," Cinderella warned. "Abby, my daughter's servant, is always by her side."

"But we will make arrangements," the prince said, taking command.

"Very well," Valdman bowed and turned to leave.

Cinderella stopped him, "Why would you do this for us? Our countries are still officially at war."

"I believe King David would approve. And even if he wouldn't, I almost had a child once. We must help our children if we can," he murmured, lost in a memory.

As he left, the royals looked at each other and embraced. Hope is always nearby and reveals itself when we least expect it.

35

Night had fallen, but Aristal was alive with laughter. The beast had been executed. The city was safe again. Why not continue the celebration through the evening? Hundreds of people gathered in the square in front of the cathedral.

Jugglers and acrobats entertained the crowd with daring feats of skill and danger. Musicians sang of the end of evil as citizens danced wildly around the pole with the witch's head.

A puppet show entertained the little ones. A happy ending was, of course, provided with the witch cut into little candy pieces and thrown to the children for consumption. Merchants sold St. Benedict medallions for protection. Food vendors hawked their delicacies to the hungry crowd. The smell of roast boart on the spit mixed with the aroma of the burnt witches.

Pickpockets moved seamlessly through the crowd, watching for soldiers as they worked the festivities. Green ladies talked to the eager young men. Under the cathedral, this grand symbol of God's mercy, there was joy, happiness, and hope.

People always think there is hope when evil has been vanquished. Sometimes, the evil itself has not been destroyed; it only takes a small respite. Often, one evil is simply replaced by another. Whether Aristal's evil was resting or being replaced, the people's joy was temporary.

The cart that held the stones used to kill Savaric and his family burst into a hundred pieces. Only the people standing nearby noticed, and they were unsure what had just happened. Then, they saw the bright red cassock partially hidden by the shattered cart. A woman screamed after she noticed the red velvet shoes. It was the bishop! More people turned to the commotion. The large square grew quickly quiet.

The cathedral guards immediately surrounded the corpse. Bishop Penk must have fallen from a great height. His eyes open, fixed in horror. His midsection was split open. The guards looked up, and the crowd followed. There on the bishop's balcony stood the beast. The creature howled, and the revelers scattered. Children were left by fleeing parents, thinking only of self-preservation. Food carts were overturned in the panic and caught fire. People were trampled and lay injured, calling for help. Chaos was everywhere.

Soldiers let their arrows fly. But the beast disappeared. Guards and soldiers flooded into the cathedral. They were met with horror at every turn.

The first victim they encountered was Father Jacob. He was thrown on the pulpit with his throat sliced open. He was leading the evening service when the attack came. The last thing he saw was the beast lunging at him. He could not beg for mercy from the creature or for forgiveness from the Lord above for his role in the death of four innocent people earlier. The worshippers could do nothing to save him. Some fled, but others remained paralyzed with fear, unable to move or cry for help.

The soldiers moved cautiously through the darkened halls. The torches had been extinguished by frightened clergy trying to hide. Usually, these passageways were filled with people busily going about church business. No one was conducting any business now. But there were many bodies. The demon must have moved at lightning speed in its desire to get to the bishop. Victims were sliced through like a knife carving a Christmas pudding.

At last, they arrived at the bishop's chambers, which led to his balcony. A dozen guards and priests lay dead on the floor. They gave their lives to protect their leader. It must have been terrifying for the mighty man to see all his protection melt away as the beast came closer.

A scream came from the hallway outside the door. A soldier had time to call for help but nothing more before dying. The men had their bows drawn and saw the beast down the hall. They let their arrows fly, but none found their mark. The shafts hit the wall as the creature disappeared down the stairway which led to the dungeon.

The small circular stairs would prove impossible to shoot an arrow. The soldiers drew their swords and moved slowly into the darkness. The sound of the creature's footsteps rushed away from the men, but they did not dare quicken their pace. The beast could hide in too many places in this cramped passageway, and it would be difficult to protect oneself.

Eventually, they arrived at the lower level of the cathedral. The church constables had quarters in this area. A holding cell where sinners were kept while waiting for trial was down the hall from the constable's quarters. The only other room on this level of the cathedral was the interrogation chamber, where Captain Umfrey and his men happily worked extracting confessions from evildoers.

Ten good men lay dead in the quarters. Two more soldiers died by the door. They must have been surprised by the intruder. The others were killed in their cots. It could only be hoped they were murdered without any knowledge of the monster in the cathedral.

Two soldiers advanced to the holding cells. One prisoner stood half-hidden in the darkness. His crime was giving a few coins to an excommunicated beggar. How can charity be a crime? But these are the times in which we live.

Earlier, he heard strange footsteps and called to be released. Then he saw the creature in the hall. The enormous grey beast looked at the imprisoned man before slowly moving on. The man sunk into the darkness, hoping it was a bad dream.

The soldiers saw the prisoner and aimed their arrows at him. They approached him when they realized he was not the target they were looking for.

"Did you see it?" one soldier asked.

The prisoner remained quiet.

"Which way did it go?" the other demanded.

The prisoner's eyes grew wide. The soldiers turned around, and the beast attacked. They died before they could call for help. The creature towered over the fallen men before turning its red eyes again to the prisoner in the cage. It seemed to smile and then raised a finger to its mouth as if to warn him to remain quiet. It disappeared down the passageway when it heard more soldiers approaching.

The soldiers got to their murdered comrades just in time to hear more screams from down the hall. They took off quickly, leaving the prisoner in his cell. The man had no desire to be rescued anyway. He was safer where he was.

They arrived at the interrogation chambers with their swords drawn. They were not a few steps into the room before they heard dripping and almost imperceptible moaning. They could barely see the details of the room until they lit the sconces on the wall. Looking up at the vaulted ceiling, they saw Captain Umfrey's assistants hanging from large meat hooks. Nothing could be done for the injured men as they slowly expired. Captain Umfrey was nowhere to be seen.

"Help!" A voice cried out from a distance.

The soldiers searched the room. At the far end, there was a grating on the floor. The metal cover was not in its place. The five remaining soldiers looked into the dark hole. The creature had killed many men. Following the beast into the tunnels would be foolish. And the men had seen enough bloodshed for one day.

"Help! Help me, please!" the voice cried again.

The men stiffened in fear. The poor man was on his own.

"May God have mercy on his soul," one of the soldiers said.

The others crossed themselves. No one would follow the beast, so they decided to remain. Nothing could be done. They replace the grate and retreated to the hall outside the interrogation room. As they walked under the men dangling above, the soldiers averted their eyes, unsure if the victims were alive, as they turned slowly in the air. They locked the door. At least the beast would not be able to enter the cathedral again. This was the most prudent thing to do. Hopefully, the man taken into the tunnels would be quiet soon. For the surviving soldiers, it was time to bury the dead.

~ 36 ~

News of the murders traveled quickly to the castle. The king called Prince John, his advisors, and his captains to the throne room. Armed soldiers lined the walls of the room.

"Report, Captain!" the king bellowed.

"Your Majesty, Bishop Penk was thrown from his balcony, and one of the priests was murdered during the evening service. Many other priests and guards were killed defending the cathedral."

"Is the attack over?"

"Yes, Sire. It appears so."

"Was this an attack by a foreign power?"

"No," the captain hesitated rocking from side to side. "From several witnesses, we believe the creature who recently attacked our soldiers is responsible."

"I thought they executed the beast earlier today, that whole business about the witch."

"That was the hope, Your Majesty, but it doesn't appear to be true."

"Where is the beast now?"

"It has escaped in the tunnels beneath the cathedral."

"Those tunnels connect to the castle."

"Yes, Your Highness."

"How will the royal family be protected?"

"A company of soldiers is assembled outside the castle walls, another within the castle walls, and a dozen men are assigned to each member of your family."

"Thank you, Captain. Let me hear from my advisors."

Edgar, a tall, thin man with beady eyes, was the first to step forward. His disdain for the commoners was evident from the sneering way he slowly pronounced his words when addressing problems with the peasantry.

"The people are frightened. Before this incident, they feared being attacked while tending their fields. Now, they will not go near the fields. I do not know how we will bring in the harvest. Their weakness will throw the kingdom into further disarray."

The king looked at the rest of his advisors.

"Do you have any solutions?"

The men remained silent. Gervase, a small, anemic man even less agreeable than Edgar, stepped forward.

"We could force the peasants to work," Gervase said, looking to the other advisors for support.

The advisors slowly agreed because they had nothing better to offer. The king was not convinced. Prince John broke the silence.

"I disagree, Father. The people are frightened and forcing them into the fields would turn their anger against us."

"What would you have us do then?"

"Captain," the prince called.

The captain of the guards stepped forward.

"Yes, Your Majesty?"

"How many of your men are assigned to my wife?"

"A dozen, sir."

"And how many of your men are assigned to Gervase here?"

"Eight, sir."

"Eight? And Princess Ella only gets a dozen? What about Edgar?

"Eight."

"What about Markin and the rest of this lot?"

"Eight. All the advisors have eight men protecting them."

"What about the Chief Housekeeper and the House Steward? Are soldiers protecting them?"

"Six, sir," the captain responded slowly.

"Does every servant have a soldier?"

"Yes, sir."

"That must make the women in the castle very happy, captain," the prince smiled slyly.

"Not all of them. You should see some of my soldiers," the captain returned the smile.

The king looked at his advisors before blurting out, "What does all this have to do with the problem of the peasants not tending their fields?"

Prince John turned to the king, "I am sorry, Father. But the captain, in his desire to keep everyone safe, has brought close to two hundred soldiers into the castle. Do we need all those men? Look at Edgar, Father. Does he really need eight soldiers for his protection?"

The king smiled, "No, Edgar does not need eight men. Two would do."

Prince John became serious. "Then have a company of soldiers watch the farmers in the fields. Let our subjects know we will protect them instead of hiding behind these walls."

The advisors seemed concerned they would no longer have eight soldiers protecting them. King Edward smiled at their discomfort.

"Anything else?" the king asked.

"You can send them out into the fields as well," John motioned to the advisors. "Let them talk to the people, hear their concerns, and report back to you. If we do not reassure our subjects, then unrest will follow, and we will have two difficulties."

"I agree," the king smiled. "Markin, have this proclaimed throughout the capital."

Markin stepped forward and bowed deeply before the king. He was exceptionally limber and enjoyed bending lower than the other advisors.

"Yes, Your Majesty."

He bowed again before leaving. The king smiled at the depth of his bows before turning to the remaining men in the room.

"But this doesn't address the bigger problem. What do we do about the monster terrorizing our kingdom?"

Everyone looked around, but no one had any answers. Prince John was unaware of these sinister events until the attack on the cathedral. He was so focused on his personal concerns that he did not have a chance to meet with the king. King Edward asked Norris, another advisor, to fill his son in.

"The first report of anything being amiss was about six weeks ago when word came about a traveler killed in Birchbank. The king dispatched his soldiers, and a large bear was killed, brought back, and displayed in the square. This calmed fears for a while until a merchant from Malbet Market was murdered, and his body was left on the steps of the cathedral. Patrols were organized to calm the population, but several weeks later, ten soldiers on patrol and several civilians were killed outside the castle gates. The city has been quiet since then."

"Until today," the prince said thoughtfully.

"Until today," Norris repeated.

"But why today? This is an escalation of hostilities," the king snapped.

"It must be the witch," Edgar said.

"We don't know if she was a witch," John dismissed the idea.

"Would this creature bring vengeance for an innocent woman? If we were not sure of the woman's guilt before tonight, the creature's actions should dispel all doubts," the king countered. Deep down, he must have felt some unease from not listening to Cinderella. "But whether she was or was not a witch is immaterial. We need to destroy the creature in our midst. Bamberger, you know the tunnels."

Bamberger stepped forward. Of all the king's advisors, he was the only one who rose from the peasantry and fought in the wars against Dandorum. He never put his desires over the needs of the king and kingdom, and the king trusted him above all.

"Yes, Your Highness. The tunnels were built with the city's foundations to serve as an escape route from Aristal in the case of a siege. In times of peace, the bishop and king could meet without going through the city streets when secrecy was needed. There are several exits beyond the city's walls as well as within the city."

"So, the creature could have come in through the tunnels?" the king questioned.

"Yes," Bamberger replied.

"How many entrances are in the castle?"

"One in the Royal crypt and one in the dungeons."

"Then let us seal every entrance and trap the beast," John ventured.

"Then how will we know when it is dead? My subjects will never accept that! We will leave one entrance open and send our soldiers to hunt the creature down, ridding the kingdom of this evil," King Edward proclaimed.

The advisors nodded in agreement. Edward smiled at his son. John had matured into a wise leader. He will make a great king one day. Edward, however, was not ready to give up his throne just yet.

"We are agreed. At morning light, we will begin walling up the exits of the tunnels. Soldiers will remain posted at each entrance until the masons complete their task. When there is no escape for the monster, we will send in our soldiers and kill it. Bamberger, you will oversee the construction."

"Yes, Sire," Bamberger said, assuring his king he would accomplish this task.

"Captain, begin training your men for their mission."

The captain stepped forward, "Yes, Your Majesty."

The creature hid in the tunnels for the next few days and made no attempt to show itself or kill again. The peasants tended their fields under the watchful eyes of heavily armed soldiers. The masons worked diligently, ensuring that whatever was in the tunnels stayed there. They built walls three feet thick. No creature on Earth or from a darker place could destroy these walls. The mortar would take a week to harden fully; until then, it was assumed that the beast would be able to break through its prison and escape. The guards needed to remain vigilant.

Though the plan had calmed the people's fears, King Edward was still troubled. The king prayed at the altar in the Royal Chapel. He believed in his heart that he was responsible for the evil in his kingdom. The kingdom is the outward manifestation of the king's ability to govern. And if the king has a flaw, somehow, the kingdom will reflect that. All the king had to do was correct his imperfections, and his country's ills would fade like the morning dew on a summer's day.

But what was the flaw? The unjustness against the witch Pesta had been resolved with her death and the return of Anne. The war with Dandorum ended with King Peter's death. Bain, it would seem, was looked upon favorably by God above. Where was his sin?

He lost himself deeply in prayer. Then, he thought this trouble started after John traveled to Dandorum to negotiate with King David. This new king was a mystery. He did not seem to desire to continue the war, but nothing was sure. He spent time here. Maybe he was a spy, as initially suspected. He knew the castle and the city intimately. He even tended to the king when he was in a weakened state. And what cure did he offer the king? That he should look inward at the sins he committed. David put the seed of doubt in his mind. And doubt is a ruler's greatest enemy.

This was an inspired ploy by King Peter, sending his own son as a spy! Even if the boy were caught, he would be ransomed, not executed! Then, all the information David gathered would return home to be used against Bain.

King Edward thought of Valdman. This most recent attack came after he arrived with John. Maybe he was responsible for this. Perhaps this was the start of a new kind of war with Dandorum.

Now everything seemed clear. That whole business with Cinderella was also a part of the plan. By confusing the lonely girl, the royal family was thrown into further disarray.

He rose quickly from his knees. This problem was not one of supernatural events or messengers of the Devil. This was simply one kingdom trying to outmaneuver another through deception. King Edward gained clarity through his prayers. When he reached the throne room, he called for his guards to bring the agitator from Dandorum to him. He would soon show his enemy how clever he could be.

Valdman stood in the presence of the king. He had witnessed this scene before when his friend David was accused of spying. The court grew quiet as the king raised his hand.

"Ambassador Valdman. I have called you here to answer questions regarding your true intentions in our kingdom."

"Your Majesty, I am here for one purpose and one purpose alone," Valdman replied.

"And what is that?" the king asked.

"To negotiate a peace between our kingdoms."

"And have you succeeded in your charge?"

"No, I have not."

"And why is that?"

"Bain has been preoccupied with certain internal matters since I arrived."

"Yes. I am interested in your role in our internal matters," the king said, his eyes narrowing as he leaned forward.

"I have no role in Bain's business except as it relates to Dandorum," Valdman replied softly to appease the king.

"Does a weakened Bain not profit Dandorum?"

"As in all discussions, it is better to come from a position of strength than weakness. But to take advantage of an adversary's troubles will only bring animosity and the desire for retribution. My wish was to devise a mutual solution to benefit our kingdoms for generations."

"Clever words come from a serpent's tongue. You went to see the bishop, and now he is dead. You argued for the freedom of the witch, and violence was released upon our city when she was justly executed. I don't know whether you have instigated these crimes or just profited from them."

"Your Majesty, I was not involved in these events. I am here to negotiate."

"So, you say. Were you also here when your king was a kitchen boy in this castle?"

"Yes, I have been with my king since he was a boy."

"Did you also work in my castle?"

"Yes, Your Majesty."

"Where did you work?"

"I worked in your gardens collecting herbs and fruits to enliven your meals."

"Did you teach David his healing arts?"

"I taught him some things, but he also learned by studying nature."

"And were you with him when he was imprisoned?"

"I have been with him almost constantly since he was young."

This was the answer that King Edward had hoped for.

"How did he escape?" The king asked, zeroing in on his target.

"I'm sorry, I don't understand your question."

"Yes, you do. You are a shrewd man. Did you help him escape?"

Valdman stood silent.

"You are at a loss for words, Ambassador Valdman. And that can only mean that you have conspired against this kingdom for many years. But I am curious: how did you do it? You could not have secreted David away through the castle gates. They are always well fortified. Was there some other method of escape unknown and therefore unguarded?"

Valdman lowered his head, not looking at the king.

"Bamberger," King Edward snapped.

"Yes, Sire," Bamberger said, stepping forward.

"How is work proceeding?"

"Very well, all the entrances have been sealed and will be fully cured in a day or two."

"Thank you for the good report. Tell me, are there any entrances on the castle grounds but not in the castle itself?"

"Yes, Your Majesty."

"Are there any in the gardens?"

"Yes, Your Majesty. There is an entrance in the groundkeeper complex."

"Would a gardener know of such a place?"

"Quite possibly."

"The possibility exists, then," the king spoke to the crowd. "That someone who worked in the gardens would know of a secret way into the dungeons where prisoners are detained. That person could use those tunnels to escape a heavily guarded castle."

"Yes, Sire."

"These tunnels also connect to the cathedral?"

"Yes," Bamberger confirmed. "That passage was originally constructed so the king and bishop could meet beyond prying eyes."

"And these tunnels served as an escape route for the creature terrorizing our city."

The advisor nodded.

"How many people knew of the tunnels before the present construction, Bamberger?"

"Only the royal family, high-ranking members of the church, and a few of your closest advisors."

"Yourself included?"

"Yes, of course."

"Would you free a convicted spy to help Dandorum?"

"No, Your Majesty," Bamberger recoiled at the thought of being disloyal.

"Of course not. Can you think of any member of the royal family who would do such a treasonous thing?"

"No, Your Majesty."

"But it does seem we have someone in our court at this moment who would free a spy of Dandorum," the king turned his gaze back to Valdman and rose dramatically. "Someone who protected that spy for many years. Someone who had intimate knowledge of the tunnel system in our capital from years of working in our gardens. And that person would benefit from our country's problems. Ambassador, that person, is you."

Valdman looked at the king. Why disagree when the king would not listen anyway? Valdman used the tunnels to free David, but had nothing to do with the kingdom's present troubles. He once thought that Bain was more ethical than Dandorum. Now, he realized that all kingdoms are the same, ruled by tyrants who create stories to fit their narratives. They executed Estrilda, and he was next in a bloody line of innocent victims that stretched back into antiquity.

"Can you explain your actions?"

"I don't have anything to say that would change your mind," Valdman said, not breaking the king's gaze.

"Very well. Presently, we do not fathom the degree to which Dandorum has meddled in our affairs, but we will find out and bring swift justice to those involved, even if it extends to King David himself. Guards, take this spy to the dungeons."

~ 39 ~

The prison where Valdman found himself was separated into ten cells by heavy iron bars. The cells were more of a temporary way station than a permanent residence. If the guards were going to hold him for a more extended period, they would have thrown him in the stone rooms behind heavy wooden doors, where unspeakable tortures take place. Valdman heard fading cries of help from those rooms as he passed down the dark, damp corridors.

They threw him in a cell before leaving to plan his execution, which would influence his method of torture. For instance, breaking a prisoner's arms and legs was better if he was to be drawn and quartered because that procedure separates the limbs from the torso. If you are burning someone at the stake, the condemned should be able to stand, at least initially, so the spectators in the back can see better.

Valdman tried to think of something other than his demise. He looked around and could see another prisoner through the darkness. The man sat on the floor in the far corner of the adjacent cell. Valdman gripped the bars, testing them for weaknesses. Finding none, he began to pace. The other prisoner chuckled.

"You better save your strength," the man chided.

"And why is that?" Valdman responded, annoyed at his present situation.

"They don't feed you well here. Worse than the cathedral. My name is Gerry," the prisoner said, extending his grimy hand.

Valdman reluctantly took Gerry's hand briefly.

"William," Valdman said, going to the far side of his cell and wiping his hand before turning to his cellmate again. "You have been in the cathedral's prisons?"

"Of course," he laughed as if he were a professional prisoner. "The cathedral's prison, the magistrate's dungeons. This is my first time here, though. It's pretty fancy, but the food is lacking."

Valdman looked at his surroundings. He would never describe his cage as fancy. "You don't like the food?"

"No, it's lacking. They haven't fed me yet!" Gerry laughed again.

No one would consider this man jolly, even though he laughed a lot. He used his laughter as a shield. His world was dark and painful, kicked and beaten by anyone who passed him as he begged for scraps of food. Arrested for every minor crime committed anywhere in his vicinity, he was locked up more than on the streets.

"How long have you been here?" Valdman asked, wasting time.

"They just brought me over yesterday after that whole mess in the cathedral," he said, crossing himself and looking up to Heaven. "They want to interrogate me. Like I have information for them."

"Do you?"

Gerry looked around to see that no one was looking. When he was sure they were alone, he let Valdman in on the secret.

"Well, I'm the only one who saw the creature and lived."

"How did that happen?"

"I was locked up. I can't get out, but it can't get in," his tone resembled a nursery rhyme. Then he became angry and filled with rage, "Let the creature kill them all. I don't care. Serves them right!"

"How will you get out of your cell after the beast kills them all?"

Gerry thought for a moment.

"Haven't figured that one out yet," he sunk down in the far corner of his cell, his passion abating.

"Good plan," Valdman shook his head.

A moment later, he heard footsteps and turned to the door. Princess Anne appeared holding a torch. She was alone. She haughtily strolled around the room, looking at the empty cells before coming to the prisoner from the cathedral. He turned his face away from the princess. Her eyes widened briefly before turning to Valdman.

"I see you have a friend."

"We just met," Valdman responded. "Although, he has some interesting views on castle security."

Anne sneered at him, "I told you I would see you punished for your impertinence!"

"Princess, I do not believe you are responsible for my present living conditions. King Edward is trying to find answers by looking in the wrong places."

"Yes, you are correct. I am not responsible for your imprisonment, but I celebrate it. And I agree with you. The ruler of this kingdom is a stupid, misguided man."

"I would never insult the king, but if you think I am not the reason for your country's misery, who is?" Valdman asked, approaching the princess.

She turned away, increasing the distance between them. He was not an ally. She had no friends here in this awful place. But this man said he knew Pesta, and she missed her mother. She turned back to him.

"When I saw you in the garden, you said you knew the witch Pesta. How is that possible? She would have killed you and fed your bones to Mardrom."

"When I met Pesta, she wasn't evil. She was a woman who was broken-hearted," Valman said compassionately.

"Liar," the princess responded. Her voice faltered as if she, deep down, believed that he might be correct.

"When I met her, she was close to death," he continued, sensing a softening in the girl's acrid demeanor. "She had taken poison because she had been betrayed. I saved her."

"How?" the princess demanded.

"I thought she was poisoned. Then I remembered my dog once ate some grasses that made it throw up. I had noticed the same plant outside Pesta's castle. I crushed it up and fed her the remedy. It purged the poison from her body, and I cared for her until she recovered."

"How did you know about that herb?"

"I knew nothing, but I figured it couldn't hurt."

"Why would you help a witch?"

"My wife was ill. I thought Pesta could do something."

"So, you saved her for selfish reasons!"

"You could say that. But most things people do have some benefit to themselves. This does not make them bad people. It makes them human. If you choose actions that purposely cause harm to others, then I imagine you could be considered a bad person."

"Did the witch help you?"

"She gave me the knowledge of flora. I was able to see a person's ailments and the herbs that could ease their pain. The other day in the garden, you did not like one of the herbs I had collected, the Devil's Claw."

Valdman studied the princess closely. She turned away from him.

"I don't understand what you are talking about," she hissed at the prisoner. "You frightened me, and I fell. You are a scary, horrible man, and I hope they kill you. I will laugh as you burn alive!"

She moved towards the door, laughing wildly. Valdman stopped her.

"*Omnia occulta revelabitur!*" he yelled, pointing his finger at her.

She turned to him. The blood drained from her face. She lunged at Valdman, dropping her torch and darkening the room. If the bars weren't there, she would have killed him. She shook the bars violently and screamed with a voice that might have come from the Devil himself. Realizing she could not reach him, she turned and flew from the room.

The two men remained in the darkness. After a moment, Gerry turned to Valdman.

"Friend, you are not very good at talking to women."

"I think I would agree with you," Valdman smiled. "And I agree with you in another way."

"What is that?"

"We might be safer in here."

"What did you say to her anyway?"

"I said *everything hidden will be revealed*."

"I could see how that would upset a woman."

~ 40 ~

A few hours after Princess Anne's visit, Valdman had more guests. Cinderella and Prince John approached his cell anxiously.

"William, I am so sorry. What can we do for you?" It broke Cinderella's heart to see her friend in this terrible place. She thought of David and the time he spent imprisoned.

"Besides restoring my freedom?" Valdman smiled. He had no desire to see Cinderella suffer because of his present state.

"We are working on that," John promised, but he knew he could not change his father's mind.

"Thank you," Valdman nodded. "My friend Gerry has not eaten since he was brought here from the cathedral yesterday."

Gerry stood up and walked into the light. He bowed in a way that made it clear he was not used to bowing.

"Your Highnesses, welcome to my home," he babbled, not knowing what to say.

John smiled. "It is lovely what you have done with the place," accepting the man's hospitality.

Cinderella took her husband's arm and smiled at Gerry. "I will make sure the cook sends you something."

"Some mutton would be nice," the starving prisoner suggested.

Gerry bowed multiple times while retreating deeper into his cell. When he hit the back wall and could go no further, he stood quietly for an awkward moment and sank to the floor. John, Cinderella, and Valdman looked at him before turning to each other.

Cinderella began, "We went to the king as soon as we heard, but he refused to release you. He is a stubborn man."

"I believe he sees an advantage in keeping you here," the prince explained. "Maybe you will be ransomed. Maybe he thinks you will be unable to negotiate after a few days of confinement. Whatever the reason, I can assure you this is not a death sentence."

"The king rules by his whims. I will not be safe until I return to Dandorum."

"I am sorry for that. John and I appreciate your efforts to bring peace to our kingdoms and the help you have promised us," Cinderella smiled.

"Your daughter paid Gerry and me a visit earlier."

Gerry harrumphed from the darkness. John and Cinderella looked at Valdman hopefully.

"Why did she do that?" the prince questioned.

"She was interested in how I knew Peșta. She was angry that the witch didn't kill me and feed my bones to Mardrom, whoever he is."

"It was a terrible beast I killed when I rescued Anne," John said with a touch of remorse.

"I believe Pesta put a spell on Princess Anne," Valdman confirmed.

"Are you sure?" Cinderella lamented.

"An *objawcelum* is a phrase that reveals spells. I said one to the Princess, and she reacted violently. Only a person enchanted would have acted in that way."

Cinderella recoiled in fear. The prince held his wife.

"Pesta was a powerful witch, and this was a dark spell she put on the Princess to make sure that even if Anne was rescued, there would be no peace for you. I am sorry," Valdman continued.

"What can we do?" asked the prince, his strong exterior beginning to crumble.

"If you can bring her servant to me, I may be able to gain knowledge of the spell and learn how to counteract it."

"We will do what you ask," the prince said, leading his wife away.

"Thank you," Valdman said thoughtfully.

"Thank you, Your Highnesses," Gerry said, appearing at the bars again, waving cheerfully at the departing couple. He looked at Valdman, "I met Cinderella!"

"Yes, you did. Gerry."

"See, William. I told you this place was fancy!"

"Yes, this is a very fancy dungeon." Valdman shook his head and smiled.

~ 41 ~

When Anne went off, she forbade Abigail from leaving the room. The poor servant paced the apartment, hoping no one would knock on the door. She would not know what to say if asked about Anne's whereabouts. What if she never came back? How long would she stay in this room before anyone looked for her? Maybe they never would! After all, she was only a servant; why would they look for her? She might die in this room from starvation!

She longed for her mistress's return. Even though Anne was cruel, she was all Abigail had. Sometimes, she wished that they had never left Pesta's castle. The rooms were dark, and life was harsh there, but it was understandable. In this kingdom, dangers appeared around every corner. And the people! They seemed nice, but Pesta warned the girls about the deception of strangers.

She liked Prince John. He protected her on their journey. He did not seem false, but Abigail had never experienced the deception of men. She was not looking forward to that day when a man would want her to be his wife. She did not know what life would be like without serving the princess, but believed that someday a man would want her to serve him. Replacing one cruel master with another was nothing to look forward to. She shrugged her shoulders. There may be something enjoyable about it.

Abigail thought about how sad Princess Ella was. She had her daughter and husband back. What more could she want? Maybe joy returns when we allow it to return. Maybe Princess Ella was holding on to her pain. It must have been hard when she was alone. Abigail hoped the princess would one day find happiness.

Anne quietly entered the room.

"Where were you?" Abigail asked.

"I am not obliged to answer your questions!" Princess Anne barked at her servant.

"I am sorry, Princess. I just worry you're in danger," Abigail said, bowing her head.

"If you must know," the princess continued, secretly wanting to talk to someone. This stupid girl was the only person she could trust in this wicked kingdom. "I went to see that horrible man who said he knew Mother Pesta."

"Did he know her?" Abigail said hopefully.

"He said he saved her. I don't believe him. Pesta wouldn't need a man to rescue her. They are all wicked liars."

"Yes, Princess." Abigail looked around the room to avoid eye contact.

"What, you disagree?" Anne fumed.

"No, Princess, but Prince John rescued us."

Prince John and Cinderella entered the room unnoticed by the girls.

"Rescued us? We would have been fine without his help. And he killed Pesta. Without him, we would still be home." She grabbed the girl and shook her roughly before tossing her to the ground.

"Home. Yes, Princess," Abigail cried softly.

"Anne! What are you doing?" Prince John said, running to the girl and making sure she was all right.

Anne looked from her father to Cinderella, standing just inside the door. She scowled at her parents.

"What are you doing here?" she growled.

"The king is about to announce the mission to kill the beast in the tunnels. We thought you would like to see it," John said.

"He could send a thousand men into the tunnels; they would never find it."

"How do you know this?" Cinderella asked, alarmed.

"Because the king is wicked, and his sins cry out against him!"

John and Ella looked at each other. Surely, she was under a powerful spell to say such terrible things about her grandfather! But their resolve was as strong as any magic.

"He is doing his best for the kingdom. And your presence is required for the ceremony," the prince reprimanded his wayward daughter.

"Being a princess is stupid. Stupid, and boring."

"You may be right, but it is our duty as part of the royal family," he smiled charitably at her.

"Well then, come on," Anne motioned to Abigail.

"Darling, may I borrow your servant?" Cinderella said to her daughter.

"Why?" Anne asked suspiciously.

"Catherine, the girl who scrubs the floors in our apartments, has taken ill. The floors haven't been cleaned in a week. I thought I might let Abby do that while you were enjoying yourself at the ceremony."

"Is there a lot of work?" Anne asked, visualizing Abigail scrubbing the floors till her fingers bled.

"Yes, Anne," Cinderella speculated.

"Will she be on her hands and knees?"

"On the cold, cold floor," Cinderella said sadly.

Anne smiled broadly. "I guess I could spare her for an hour or two. Now, father, let's go hear the king's tedious speech," she said, taking John's arm and leading the prince out of the room.

After Anne and John left, Cinderella smiled reassuringly at the servant. The girl had a pretty face, but her insecurity overshadowed her beauty. Abigail bowed her head, avoiding the princess' eyes.

~ 42 ~

The king rose from his throne to address his troupes. One hundred brave soldiers stood at attention in the center of the large hall. Many lords and ladies called to the capital to witness the king's future triumph over the creature were in attendance. The castle staff were also on hand.

The king's eyes narrowed in annoyance as he noticed his son and Anne quietly join his party late. They should have been here at the start of this auspicious ceremony. The king would address this matter later, but now, he had more significant issues to tackle. Edward turned to the soldiers.

"Men, our kingdom is in your hands. Evil has come to our city and has found a home. It feeds on helpless women who were nothing but good wives and mothers or innocent children, playing carelessly in the streets just beyond their mother's watchful gaze. It has attacked your mothers, wives, daughters, fathers, and sons. All innocent victims."

Anne shifted and let out a barely perceptible sigh. John looked at her to stifle any further signs of disapproval.

"What?" she grumbled at her father.

"Quiet, please," he whispered.

"He lies. No women or children were killed. I've heard the reports, soldiers and terrible men who probably deserved it," she raised her voice just enough to let the queen and nearest advisors notice.

John looked at the king. This was not the time to correct his daughter's behavior.

"My dear friends," the king continued. "You have been tasked with killing the creature that has committed these crimes. We have trapped it in the tunnels beneath our city. And now we will hunt it down and destroy it once and for all, sending it back to Hell from whence it came. Yes, a creature as evil as this must have come from Hell itself, with its father being none other than the Devil."

A few soldiers shifted uncomfortably. They did not sign up for a fight with the Devil. They would lay down their lives against other soldiers, but to take on the beast itself seemed a little unfair. Some looked to their fellows while others stared at their shoes. Only the men in the first few rows continued to look at the king unflinchingly.

"You have been divided into groups. Each group has been assigned a different sealed tunnel entrance. Your task is to make it to that entrance expeditiously. If you encounter the beast on the way, destroy it. If it manages to elude you as you reach your destination, you will fight your way back to the original entrance. Nothing will be able to get away. When you emerge from the tunnels dragging the carcass of our enemy, you will be heroes, and I will forever be in your debt."

The soldiers were divided into seven groups. The first group would attempt to make it to the bishop's study, where a large group of priests and cathedral guards were murdered. The next group would try to reach the interrogation chambers in the cathedral, where the creature escaped, dragging Captain Umphrey with him. The third group would go to the groundskeeper's cottage in the royal gardens. The fourth group's destination was the royal crypt in the castle. The fifth group to the tavern in the Malbet Market, which had an entrance in the cellars. This entrance was thought to be the one the creature used when it killed the poor merchant. The sixth group would attempt to reach the entrance under High Bridge by the west entrance to Aristal. The last group was assigned to reach Fredrics Folly, located less than a mile outside the city overlooking the river. The folly had long ago been abandoned and was crumbling from neglect. The king's advisors believed this entrance might have been the one the creature initially used to access the city.

The court burst into applause to thank the soldiers risking their lives to secure the kingdom's safety. The lords and ladies, in their fancy outfits, would not risk their lives for anything, but they could appreciate those who would, especially when they felt their power slipping away.

The courtiers continued their cheers as the king, followed by the queen and his advisors, mingled with the soldiers to wish them Godspeed. Prince John motioned to his daughter to follow the advisors, but she remained planted in her spot. She would not condescend to greet these soldiers who were about to meet their doom. It was a waste of energy, and she could spend her time better by abusing a servant somewhere.

"Father," she asked thoughtfully. "Where is Abigail?"

"She is scrubbing floors, I imagine, as your mother has suggested. Why?"

"Because it appears that all the other servants are here watching Grandfather give his little speech. Why wouldn't Mother and Abigail be required to be bored as well?"

"Would you prefer your maid to be a part of such a momentous celebration?"

"No, Father, I suppose not."

"I thought so. Now, let us wish the troupes well. Those men probably have never seen a princess as beautiful as you."

She brightened, "Do you think so, Father?"

Prince John returned her smile, "Why, Anne, you are just about the prettiest girl in the whole kingdom!"

"Just about?" the girl pouted.

"You are the prettiest girl in the whole kingdom," he extended his hand.

She smiled coquettishly, "Very well, Father, I guess I could be nice to a few rough boys before they go off to battle."

She took his hand and then wrapped her arm around his arm. They approached the soldiers. Prince John smiled and thought, *maybe she is not so different from other girls her age, a little spoiled, but a simple compliment will always melt a cold exterior.*

$$\sim 43 \sim$$

The damp smell of decay and urine filled Simon's nostrils. The soldier's eyes stung with the stench. Slowing his breathing allowed him to breathe the foul air without gagging. He squinted until his eyes became accustomed to the dark tunnel. Just as he prepared himself to proceed, he was pushed from behind.

"Go on then," the soldier behind him said, laughing.

Simon stepped into the tunnel with a torch in one hand and his sword in the other. At that moment, he doubted his decision to volunteer for this mission. He grew up around where Alard, the potter, lived. The poor man! His mother still lived there. How would it be if something happened to her?

Those thoughts disappeared immediately when he stepped into a putrid puddle, losing his balance in the black slime.

"What's the matter, Simon? Not up for the task?" Simon's tormentor, Quince, scoffed.

Simon smiled as he thought of pushing Quince into the creature's hungry jaws. That man had been irritating him since he became a castle guard. Just because his uncle was a guard, doesn't mean he could treat others cruelly. And what happened to his uncle? Quince never mentions that his uncle left the castle in disgrace after impregnating one of the queen's maids. They were dismissed and are living in shame in Toltin! Toltin, of all places! Simon hoped the beast was hungry when it came to Quince.

The tips of his soft shoes curled under and made walking awkward. Simon moved in starts and stops from the jabs in his back by the dunce behind him.

The joking and jeering stopped as the men moved deeper into the tunnel. They needed each other. Simon's fantasies of an eviscerated Quince would only resume if they both survived.

The narrow passage made arrows inadvisable. With outstretched arms, one could easily touch both walls and the ceiling. The light from the torch extended no further than five yards from Simon. If the beast charged the soldiers at full speed, it would be on them before they could defend themselves. So, the men proceeded slowly, with swords extended into the darkness.

Simon's group moved into the tunnel first. Their job was to make their way to the bishop's study. Each group would reach their destination and await instructions given to the captains through a small hole left open in the sealed tunnel entrance. The gap was only as wide as a finger or two, so written notes could be passed inside, but the beast could not get out. If the creature managed to evade the soldiers, all the groups, as one, would work their way back to the one entrance left open. This would ensure that nothing could slip by them.

At first, the expedition seemed easy. There were so many men in the tunnel that nothing could defeat the united army. But as the troupes moved farther, each group broke off to follow a different path to their destination and soon were all alone, small pockets of light in the vast darkness.

~ 44 ~

Cinderella led Abigail quickly away from the main floors where they could be seen. Her eyes darted from side to side as though they were on a secret mission.

"Where are you taking me?" Abigail said, anxiously following Cinderella down the steps leading to the subterranean rooms of the castle.

Cinderella did not answer her.

"Your rooms are on the upper floors on the castle's east side," Abigail continued, trying to fill the silence. She began to worry.

Cinderella's quietness implied they were doing something forbidden. Suddenly, the princess stopped, turned, and looked directly into the poor girl's eyes, "I promise you everything will be all right. I hope you can trust me, Abigail."

Abigail managed a meager smile and lowered her eyes. What right did she have to question the princess? "I do, Your Highness."

There was something about this servant that reminded Cinderella of herself. She was a good person, alone in the world, forced to serve a mean-spirited master. She would protect this girl to the best of her abilities.

"Good," Cinderella turned, continuing her rapid pace. "It is through this door."

Before them stood a solid wooden door guarded by a well-armed soldier. On their approach, he opened the door and bowed slightly to the princess, but his eyes narrowed as he watched the girl.

"Thank you," Cinderella said, entering the prison.

Abigail lowered her eyes as she passed the guard. She looked at the room's horrible condition and gasped. "I'm afraid I would have to work here for more than an hour to clean this place, Your Highness." She bit her lip.

Cinderella smiled at the girl, "Don't worry. I didn't ask you here to scrub floors."

She approached a cell, and Valdman came into the light. When Abigail saw him, she turned to the locked door. She was trapped. The blood pounded in her head. She turned back and screamed when she saw Gerry's toothy grin in the cell next to Valdman's.

"Good day, Princess," Gerry said, bowing deeply, a little less awkward than his previous bow. He was getting used to this hobnobbing with royalty in the castle dungeons. "And who is your pretty friend?" he said in a mildly disturbing manner.

Cinderella smiled cordially, "This is Abigail. Gerry, would you mind giving us a moment?" she said, indicating Valdman.

"Of course, Your Majesty." He bowed and moved to the far end of his cell.

"Hello, Abigail," Valdman said as he studied the girl.

"You are the man from the garden. The man who knew Pesta," she stammered.

"Yes, Abigail. I am. How did you get to be Princess Anne's servant?"

Abby's breathing became rapid and shallow. She had nowhere to go. Then she looked at the princess. Cinderella smiled, and Abigail's breathing returned to normal.

"Don't worry, Abby. We want to help," Cinderella soothed the frightened servant.

"All right," she said, taking a deep breath. "My parents left me out in the forest. They didn't want me. After several days, I found Pesta's castle. She invited me in and protected me. The princess needed a friend, and when I was ready, I became her servant. Orphans don't remain friends with princesses for long," she said sadly.

"Did Pesta put a spell on the Princess?"

Abigail became frightened again. How could he know?

"No, why would Mother Pesta do that?" she said, backing away.

Cinderella held the girl steady and led her back to Valdman.

"She acted bewitched in the garden when she saw this," he pulled the Devil's Claw from his satchel.

Abigail's eyes rolled up into her head, and she collapsed. Cinderella caught her and gently placed her on the floor. Valdman put the herb away. He looked at Cinderella.

"Interesting," he said, staring at the unconscious girl.

"What does it mean, William?" Cinderella asked.

"Well, it means that both girls are under Pesta's spell."

"But why?"

"I don't know. Quickly, put this in the girl's pocket," he held out a small green twig with dangling white flowers.

"What is it?" Cinderella asked as she put the twig in Abigail's pocket.

"It is Solomon's Seal. It will protect her until we uncover what is going on."

"Do you have some for Anne?"

"Her reaction was much more violent than Abigail's. It might be too dangerous. But we will figure this out," Valdman reassured Cinderella.

Abigail opened her eyes slowly and smiled at Cinderella, who was kneeling beside her.

"I'm sorry, Princess. I don't know what happened," she apologized, struggling to get up.

"Don't worry. You just lost your balance for a moment. We probably should get you back."

"Thank you, Princess."

"We shouldn't mention this to Anne. She might be upset that you fainted."

"Yes, Your Highness."

Cinderella turned to Valdman and nodded before leading the girl away. Valdman watched as they left the room. Gerry joined Valdman at the bars. They looked at the door. Finally, Gerry broke the silence.

"Nice girl, that Abby."

"Yes."

"A little weak in the knees."

"Yes," Valdman replied, trying to concentrate on what spell Pesta might have put on the girls.

"You think I got a chance with that one?"

Valdman turned to his fellow prisoner. "No, I don't think you have a chance with that one! You spend more time in dungeons than you do out in the sunshine. Where would you go? What would you do? No, I don't think you would have a chance!"

Gerry sighed and walked to the far corner of his cell, "I was just asking. No harm in that, is there?"

Valdman shook his head, "No, Gerry, there is no harm in that."

$$\sim 45 \sim$$

Simon's group arrived at the bishop's study in just over an hour. The journey would have taken less than ten minutes if they were not afraid of being attacked by the Devil's spawn at every turn. The soldiers breathed a sigh of relief, but that faded quickly. The soldiers were as far from the other groups as possible, with no hope of reinforcements if they were attacked.

The captain made his way to the small opening in the wall. He broke the beam of light through the hole, returning the room to darkness.

"Halo," Captain Terric called to the outside world. "Halo!"

The soldiers waited without taking a breath. If someone answered, they would feel a connection to that safe world. But no one responded. The men turned to the tunnel and raised their torches to dispel the darkness.

"Captain Terric," a voice from the other side finally answered.

The soldiers in the tunnel jumped at the sound. Terric looked disgusted at his men before returning to the opening.

"Yes, we are here," Terric confirmed.

"Good. This is Dennis. Did you see anything?"

"Dennis, huh?" Terric harrumphed, showing his disappointment that he had gotten one of the stable boys as his messenger. "No, all was quiet. Have you heard from the other groups?"

"All groups have reported except Rensen. That group had the longest way to go. We expect them to check in any moment."

"Well, what do we do until then?" Terric snorted. "Have a tea party?"

"I'm sure you will get the order to proceed presently."

Terric turned to his men and spit on the ground. "Dennis, huh? I bet they didn't send Rensen or Bouch a stable boy! What does a soldier have to do in this army to get a little respect around here?"

His eyes narrowed as he looked deep into the tunnel. He saw nothing but knew something waited in the void. Then he heard it, soft but clear, a call for help. Terric returned to the wall protecting Dennis and barked, "There's something out there. Someone is calling for help. We're going to investigate."

"I don't think you should move from your position. I mean, you don't have orders to proceed, Captain Terric!" the voice insisted.

"Sod off!" the captain grumbled as he raised his sword and faced the darkness. "Come on, men."

~ 46 ~

"What did he say?" Prince John asked his wife after leaving Anne in her rooms.

"Valdman said they were both enchanted by Pesta."

"Why? How?"

"He didn't know. Do you know anything?"

"Why would I know anything?" John asked defensively.

"On the journey back, after you rescued them. Did you notice anything?"

"Ella, I don't know. I was so upset that I couldn't think straight."

"Upset about what, John?"

The prince averted his eyes from his wife. She touched his shoulder, and he moved away. After a moment, he turned back to her.

"I am ashamed."

"What is wrong, my darling?" she said, touching his face gently.

"I did not like who I was bringing back. I spent so many years away from you, and the girl I rescued was mean, angry, and vicious. The way she treated Abigail; how could our child be so terrible?'

"But darling, don't you see, she isn't our daughter. She is enchanted, which makes her act differently. That is not our daughter, but we will get our daughter back. I trust Valdman. He is a wise man. He will help us. And I trust you. Together, we will figure this out."

"But what if we can't?"

"We will."

"How do you know that?"

"Love is stronger than hate, and hatred is the power behind Pesta's spell."

"Do you love me, Ella?"

"I do, John."

"Sometimes, on my journey, I thought you had forgotten me."

"I could never do that."

"Did you ever think I had forgotten about you?"

She looked at him, and tears welled up in her eyes. At first, a single tear, then a steady stream.

"Yes, John. I thought you had forgotten me."

"You were the only thing I remembered. Everything else was a blur. The way you danced with me."

"Sometimes I wondered if that dance was all we had."

"No, that dance, that dance, there was nothing besides you. I did not see the crowds. I did not hear the music. You were everything to me. The time you were distraught and came to dinner in servant's clothes. I did not know what to do. I never knew what to do with you, but I knew I loved you with all my heart."

"I didn't think I deserved to be your wife. I was only a poor servant girl."

"You deserve much more than I could give you. That was why my quest was so important. I could not tell you how I felt but could show you how much you meant to me by bringing Anne back. Then, when she was less than I had imagined, I thought that maybe this was symbolic of our life together, big and grand but empty inside, and I was disheartened."

"Oh," Cinderella could not look at her husband.

"But then I saw you again, and the world went away. There was nothing, just you, and you were all I needed. And I knew that if you still loved me and you would let me love you, the world would be, well, we could be...happy."

"I could never stop loving you, John."

"Nor I you."

"That night in the servant's dress..."

"Yes?"

"I just wanted you to listen and understand."

"I will try to do better in the future." He smiled at her.

"We'll see." And she smiled back.

~ 47 ~

The men moved slowly down the narrow corridor. At times, the cry for help seemed just around the corner, and at other times, far away. The quality of the voice also changed. Sometimes, it was like a little girl; at other moments, it sounded like a woman.

Terric slowly began to believe that the voice was not human at all and could be a trap.

"Keep your guards up, men," he said, trying to sound commanding.

But his authority had already faded. The soldiers didn't know what they would find in this tunnel, but they knew it wasn't a damsel in distress. And then the voice faded, leaving only silence. The men continued for several more minutes, no one daring to speak.

Abruptly, Terric stopped. The soldiers held up their torches to reveal Captain Umfrey impaled on a wall sconce. The chief torturer ended his time on earth being tortured himself. The metal frame pierced his chest, a look of terror on his face.

Two soldiers crossed themselves and said a silent prayer for the deceased. Quince moved his torch closer to the body. "Here, what's that?"

"What's what?" Terric demanded.

"On the wall, below his finger. It looks like writing."

The men moved closer, studying the markings written in blood. The fact that none of the men knew how to read made the matter more difficult. Terric gave his men a disgusted look. Whatever the dead man was trying to communicate was lost to them.

"Well, there is nothing here, men. Let's get back to the study and await further orders."

Turning to go, they came face to face with the creature. Simon was the first to feel the sting of its claws. Blood poured from his face as he struck the wall. No longer would Simon wish for his tormentor's death because Quince died immediately after. The beast threw Quince onto the men who were holding out their swords behind him. Their blades, blocked by their dead comrade, were now useless for attack. Following quickly behind its human shield, the beast slashed and tore at the soldiers. No one could plunge their sword into the beast's heart, and no one would be going back to a hero's welcome. The beast went through the group, striking man after man down. Their weapons clanking sharply to the ground, the flames of the torches were as quickly extinguished as the men. The beast stood over the bodies, slowly breathing, surveying its gruesome work before disappearing in search of another group of doomed soldiers.

$$\sim 48 \sim$$

Terric's was not the first group to die in the tunnels. Captain Rensen and his men were attacked before they made it halfway to Fredrics Folly. The creature surprised them, killing Rensen first. With their captain gone, the remaining soldiers hesitated before attacking the beast. It, however, killed without hesitation. They died in a moment, and the beast moved on.

The king waited for all the groups to report before giving his order to proceed. As time passed and Rensen failed to report, the king began to worry. The courtiers shifted where they stood as the tension mounted.

"Where is Rensen, Captain?" the king demanded.

The captain, his body rigid, had no answer for the king.

"I'm sure they will report in shortly."

"Shortly is not good enough. Are the rest of the groups ready?"

"Yes, sir."

A soldier came in and whispered something to the captain.

"It appears that one of the groups left their destination. They heard a cry for help."

"Who was in command?"

"Captain Bouch, Your Majesty."

"What was his destination?"

"The High Bridge entrance, Your Majesty."

Bamberger stepped to the king's side.

"Pardon me, Your Majesty, if those groups confronted the monster and have not been heard from."

"We can assume they are dead," King Edward said barely above a whisper.

Bamberger nodded but did not go back to his place. After a moment, the king looked at him again.

"Is there anything else?"

"Yes, Your Majesty. Those were the two entrances furthest away from the castle. Which means..."

"That the creature is moving closer."

"Yes, Your Majesty."

"Let us hope our soldiers can stop it."

"Yes, Your Majesty."

The creature seemed to understand where each group would be and knew the tunnels better than the soldiers sent in to kill it. The plan was terrible in theory and tragic in reality.

Simon woke up and struggled to see in the darkness. He didn't hear any sounds. His head throbbed from the impact with the tunnel wall. Simon touched his face. The blood had already dried. He must have been out for a while. The tunnel was so dark he could hardly see, but he knew where he was. And he knew he was alone.

Simon slowly crawled around, trying to find something recognizable. He found a body. Leaning in, he could barely make out that it was Quince. Blood covered his chest. Simon shook him, but Quince did not respond. His tormentor was dead, just a heap of flesh and bones. Simon felt neither happiness nor sorrow for the man who made him feel so much anger when he lived.

Simon moved on, crawling to the next body. He found Drapper, Ferrier, and Stokes. Simon recognized Captain Terric by the red sash he always wore when going into battle but could not find his head. They were all here. They were all dead.

He leaned against the cold, damp wall and cried silently, too afraid to let the beast hear him. He was covered with his comrades' blood, wishing the beast had killed him as well so he would never know this pain.

Then, his mind focused, and he stopped crying. "I must warn them," he said barely above a whisper. Not that anyone was listening, but when a desire is so strong within you, sometimes it sneaks out.

But how to warn the other soldiers? He had no answer. He knew, however, that he could not help anyone if he remained in place. Simon started crawling. He wanted to get away from this carnage, He wanted to help any soldiers in this terrible place. He wanted to get home. If he was in the back of his group when they were attacked, and Captain Terric was in the front, then the castle must be in front of him. Even if he guessed incorrectly, maybe he could find another group.

Simon crawled until he heard a sound that made his stomach turn, a cry for help. At times, the cry seemed just around the corner; at other times, it was far away. Sometimes, it seemed as if it were a little girl or an older woman. The creature was luring another group of soldiers to their deaths!

He called out, but his voice was weak because of his injuries. "Stop, stop! Don't go! It's a trap!"

No one responded. Simon quickened his pace, but before he could reach the group, he heard the screams from soldiers as they were attacked. The battle lasted only a few moments. And then there was silence. No cheers of victory from the men meant that they were all dead.

Simon felt his heart drop. If it wasn't dead, the beast would be hunting again. Maybe it heard Simon's warning and would be looking for him. Simon stopped and waited in the silence. He slowly laid down and listened. An eternity might have passed. Then he heard the approaching sounds of the animal's paws splashing in the puddles on the floor. The beast was coming for him!

Simon felt his heart pounding in his chest, but he remained frozen on the ground. As the creature approached, he held his breath. It sniffed and snorted inches above his head. It smelled the dried blood of Simon's comrades, which covered him. The beast hesitated as if it was confused by the single corpse separated from the other bodies when it heard more soldiers. They were closer to the castle now, and the soldiers were more tightly grouped. The creature turned and headed into the darkness.

~ 50 ~

The atmosphere in the throne room no longer seemed like a victory celebration. Many people stood around in the room's deepest corners, talking in frightened whispers. Some of them managed to slip away, hoping to leave the capital before the creature attacked again.

Hours had passed since the king lost contact with Rensen and his men. The other groups also disobeyed their orders not to investigate the cries for help. It would have done them little good to stay where they were told. The beast would have come for them eventually. The tunnels were silent, and the silence was terrifying.

"Your Majesty, Your Majesty," Bamberger repeated to shake the king from his dreadful thoughts.

"What," the king responded without hope.

"The mission appears to have failed."

"Yes, Bamberger. We are at the creature's mercy," the king faltered as the word stuck in his head. "Mercy? It has no mercy."

"But maybe there is some hope."

Prince John returned to the hall after speaking with Cinderella. The joy he had a moment before left him when he saw his father slumped on the throne.

"What is it, father?"

"It appears, John, that we have failed. Bamberger was about to tell me why there is hope."

Father and son looked to the advisor. Bamberger hesitated a moment before beginning.

"The beast is still in the tunnels. There is only one way out. If we work quickly, we could seal it in. It will eventually die of starvation."

"The soldiers could not kill it?" John questioned.

"No. They were not strong enough."

"Are they all dead?" John looked at the king.

"We believe so."

"You believe? If there are some survivors, you'll be sentencing them to death at the creature's hands!"

The king sank into his chair. He could not answer his son. Bamberger tried to rescue him.

"Pardon me, Your Highness, but they are soldiers. They knew the dangers. And if we seal the tunnel, the creature can do no more harm. We will have rid the kingdom of this evil, maybe not in the way originally planned, but the end will have been accomplished. We must act quickly."

The king remained quiet. He never had any problem making royal decisions before. Now, he seemed childlike, incapable of answering the simplest question.

"Father."

"No, Bamberger is right. We must act quickly to preserve our kingdom."

"But, Father, the men. Surely there must be another..."

"No!" the king bellowed, assuming control again. "I am the king! And I do what is right for my people. They were willing to go into battle and die for me. And that is what they will do. Die for king and country because Bain will never fall to such evil!"

Everyone stopped whispering and turned to the king with hope and love. He would do what was necessary to preserve their way of life, and they cheered for their brave, wise ruler.

"Bamberger, do what must be done," the king whispered while waving at the crowd. He felt like their ruler again.

"Yes, Your Majesty," Bamberger replied.

John bowed to his father and left the room. The king did not notice.

~ 51 ~

Simon spent hours crawling in the tunnels. After finding three more groups of dead soldiers, he realized that warning them would have had no good consequence. He decided to make his way to the castle and alert the king. Maybe there would be enough soldiers in the castle to kill the beast once and for all.

Animals often roll themselves in the excrement of other animals to disguise their scent. Simon had the blood of his fellow soldiers splattered all over him. He rolled in the sewage on the tunnel floor to further confuse his scent. He found a forgotten cape from long ago, probably lost by an emissary from the king or bishop on a secret mission. It smelled worse than anything Simon had already rolled in, so he held onto it.

His eyes had grown accustomed to the darkness. In some areas, light seeped through the drainage holes from the streets above when the tunnels rose to just below street level. But when there was no light, Simon used the walls to navigate his way.

He no longer heard the cries for help. He no longer listened for the cries for mercy. The tunnels remained silent except for the occasional drip of water. He knew there were no longer men to kill. He and the beast were the only living things down there.

But he didn't fear the creature either. He felt as if he were already dead. What further harm could the beast do to him? This new belief did not make him reckless. It made him more focused. Simon moved quickly and quietly.

Time in darkness disappears. There was nothing to tie him to the world above or to life. He had no idea how long he searched the lonely tunnels for rescue. Soon, his mind began to play games on him. He heard his mother calling.

"Simon, Simon, hurry home. Your dinner's waiting," his mother beckoned.

Was this some sort of terrible magic? He dared not answer his mother for fear of calling attention to himself. But her voice seemed to come from a turn in the tunnel, so he followed his mother's voice.

Moments later, he saw Alard down one of the paths when the tunnel divided. The dead man waved and moved slowly away. He followed Alard until the ghost's light faded.

These apparitions wanted to help him. They wanted him to warn the king and save the kingdom. They gave him hope that he might survive this terrible mission.

Simon waited for otherworldly instruction the next time the tunnel split but received none. Did they lead him to this place just to abandon him? Then he heard the creature behind him and threw himself on the ground, covering himself with the cape, waiting for the end. The beast approached but passed him by. The smell from the cape fooled the creature. Simon remained undercover for endless moments. In the stillness, he listened. He thought he was imagining things again, but the splashes in the puddles sounded like footsteps. He wanted to peer out from his hiding place to discover what man would walk with the creature, but he dared not, waiting for the tunnel to return to silence.

He slowly rose to his feet. Two paths were in front of him. He did not know which route the creature took or which was the quickest way to the castle. He felt desperate. Turning away from his choices, the eviscerated Quince stood before him, looking at Simon with regretful eyes. Simon stifled a scream, knowing that the beast remained nearby, but threw himself against the wall to escape from his tormentor. Who knows? Maybe Quince would continue to abuse Simon even in the afterlife?

Quince was not interested in harming Simon. The spirit passed him and took the path to the right. Maybe this was Quince's chance to redeem himself before being judged by the Heavenly Court. Simon hoped for the best and followed the regretful ghost. At times, the spirit would stop, unsure how to proceed. It listened for instructions. Simon listened as well but heard nothing.

It occurred to Simon that if this was Quince's way of doing penance for his sins, then Simon should forgive him. How could he expect mercy from the Heavenly Father if he were unwilling to give mercy himself?

He could not believe it but heard himself say, "Brother Quince, I forgive you all your sins against me."

Immediately, the ghost disappeared. "S'bones! I should have waited to release the bugger! At least until he got me out of this godforsaken place!"

Simon did not curse often, but when he did, he was fluent. He could have saved his words for another time because right behind where Quince's head was a moment ago was a flame from a candle suspended in midair. On closer inspection, Simon saw the candle through a crack in the wall facing him. He moved to the wall and pushed it. The wall slid open to reveal a chapel, and the candle burned right below a statue of Mother Mary. He had made it back to safety!

He closed the wall and stumbled to the first pew. This was the most beautiful room he had ever seen. And the Holy Mother seemed to lift Simon's pain away. He collapsed on the bench and wept, thanking God for his salvation. Almost immediately, his prayers were interrupted.

"Oy! What are you doing there!" the soldier demanded, pointing his spear at Simon.

Simon stood up and held out his hands to show he was unarmed. "I was one of the soldiers sent to kill the beast. But they're dead. They're all dead. I found my way back to warn the king."

"How did you get here? All the entrances have been sealed," said the guard, not believing him.

"The entrance is right here behind this wall," Simon moved slowly and opened the hidden passageway.

The soldier stared into the darkness before closing the door. "We better get you to the king. Pwah, you stink to high heaven! What have you been rolling in?"

"You don't want to know."

"Well, I can't bring you before the king smelling like that. Come with me, and we'll clean you up."

Simon was safe again. He smiled as he followed the soldier.

$$\sim 52 \sim$$

The old king was more troubled than usual because of the terror in the capital. He entered the private chapel, lost in thought. He often found himself in this peaceful place when the world's worries would give him little rest. No one interrupted his solitude here, and he was allowed a few moments of peace.

He smiled as he entered the room and sat in the pew closest to the statue of Mary, for he usually prayed to her. He closed his eyes and took a deep breath. A foul odor overcame his senses, and he opened his eyes, looking around for what produced such a stench.

Discovering nothing in the chapel's darkness, he returned to his prayers.

"Holy mother, please give me guidance. I no longer know what..."

His prayers were again interrupted by approaching footsteps. He stood, hoping a guard had come in with a report on the creature's demise or that it had finally been walled in and would no longer trouble his kingdom. But there was no one bringing good news to the king. No one was there. Once more, the troubled man returned to his prayers.

He heard the sound a second time, and he rose in anger, turning to the intruder, ready to berate him. Then he saw his granddaughter, and his mood softened. He breathed a sigh of relief.

"Why are you up so late, my child?" the king asked, smiling at the girl.

"Yes, I am," she answered.

"What?" he asked, confused.

"I am your child," she responded.

He looked around. Two torches were the only lights in the room. The king thought that she may have confused him with his son.

"I am the king, my dear," he said.

"And what are you praying for, my king?"

"I am praying for what I always pray for peace in my kingdom."

"Your god is deaf."

"What?"

"Mother Pesta told me how evil you were, and now I understand. Even your own God won't listen to you!"

"What?"

"You bring evil upon your kingdom and then seek salvation from some higher being. Your God doesn't care because he is deaf to the prayers of wicked people. You will have to pay for your sins with your blood."

"I don't care if you are my granddaughter; you will suffer for your blasphemous speech."

"I am your daughter," the girl screamed.

"You are my granddaughter, Princess Anne!" the king roared in reply.

She stepped from the shadows, unafraid of the old man's threats.

"My mother was Pesta. You deceived her for a trinket and left her with child. She hated the thing growing inside her and cursed it. She prayed for death. The gods did not listen to her prayers either. She survived, but the child inside her was deformed. When the abomination was born, Pesta named her Mardrom for the nightmare it was. I am your child, father. I am Mardrom."

As she approached the king, she transformed into her true form, revealing her evil nature. Terror filled the old king's heart as he realized his sins had returned to destroy him. He did not run or call for help. Maybe by sacrificing himself, the evil would leave his kingdom. But the beast would make no deals, and her bloodlust would not be satisfied with his death.

"What's the matter, father? Won't you kiss your daughter?"

She lunged at the old man who could not defend himself. Mardrom did not end the king's life instantly but slit his throat so that he would die slowly, unable to cry for help. She stood over him, watching his life cover the chapel floor. She usually killed quickly with joyful ferocity. But this was also enjoyable, watching her victim helplessly, hopelessly drift away.

"Don't worry, Father, after you join Mother Pesta in Hell, I will kill the others. No one will live because they profited from your evil acts. And when justice has been extracted, I will return to my castle and hide myself from the deceitful world of men."

The king died as he listened to Mardrom's plans under the statue of the holy mother, blindly looking down on the bloody scene.

~ 53 ~

After Simon was bathed and dressed, the guard took Simon to the throne room. The king was not there. Bamberger was finalizing plans to wall up the last entrance to the tunnels with the captain of the guard.

"Excuse me, your Excellency."

"What is it," Bamberger replied in a dismissive voice.

"I'm sorry to disturb you, but this man said he was with one of the groups sent to kill the beast."

"That is impossible. No one has exited the tunnels. A hundred men guard the entrance to stop anything that comes out."

"I'm sorry, sir, but I didn't come out where I entered."

"He lies. There is no other exit," Bamberger gruffly replied.

"I'm sorry, sir," said the guard. "But I saw it myself."

"Where is it?"

"In the chapel," Simon said.

"Go to the king's apartments. Quickly!"

"Yes sir," the guard nodded to Simon before heading to find the king.

"Captain!"

The captain of the guards stepped forward.

"Send some men to bring the prince to the chapel and others to watch the Queen and Princess Ella. Take twenty of your men and accompany me to the chapel immediately."

"Yes, sir!"

~ 54 ~

By the time Prince John arrived at the chapel, Bamberger and his men had blocked it off. The soldiers parted as John approached, but Bamberger stood in his way. Tears were in his eyes.

"What is it," the prince demanded.

"It is the king," Bamberger replied solemnly.

The prince pushed him aside and entered the chapel. His eyes were fixed on the blessed mother. Red specks on her white alabaster dress. He saw his father at the front of the chapel.

The king, his father, was no longer alive. A hundred thoughts passed through his mind. *The last thing he did was yell at me. I never told him goodbye. I never told him that I loved him. Did I love him? When was the last time that he said he loved me? Did he love me, or was I just a way of continuing his reign? What will our kingdom do without him? Does that make me the king? I am not ready to be king. I do not want to be king.*

This would have continued indefinitely because death gives us no answers, only more questions. Bamberger broke the silence.

"Excuse me, Your Majesty."

"Yes," the prince responded.

"The soldier who found the entrance is here."

"Thank you. Bring him in. And Bamberger, please have some men bring my father to the doctor to prepare his body for burial," his voice was soft and far away.

"Yes, Your Majesty."

"Your Majesty," the prince repeated softly. "Also," he paused for a moment. "Please have someone clean my father's blood from the floor."

176

"Yes, Your Majesty."

This was not a time for reflection or mourning. There would be time for that later. Now, the prince needed to become the king, whether he wanted to or not.

"Thank you." John looked up and saw Simon. "Please come here."

"I'm sorry, Your Majesty. I wanted to warn the king. I'm sorry."

"What is your name?"

"Simon, Your Majesty."

"And you alone survived in the tunnels, Simon? How do you explain that?"

"I guess I am just lucky, Your Majesty."

"You must be. And you found a secret passage in this room?"

"Yes, Your Majesty." Simon walked past the prince and opened the hidden door.

"Bamberger," the prince called.

"Yes, Sire."

"Did you know of this entrance?"

"No, Sire."

"Then can we assume there are other entrances you do not know about?"

"Yes, Sire."

"Then this castle is not safe."

"No, Your Majesty, it is not. Might I suggest..."

"No, you may not. Send men for the queen. I will get my wife. Simon, let's hope your luck continues. Please bring Princess Anne and her servant Abigail. We will gather everyone in the great hall. We will be able to protect them there."

~ 55 ~

Simon pounded on Princess Anne's door.

"Princess, Princess? The creature is in the castle! Your father sent me to bring you safely to the Great Hall."

Silence.

His heart sank. Fearful that the beast had already hurt the princess, he kicked open the door and rushed in with his sword drawn.

Abby was curled up in the chair, rocking with tears streaming down her cheeks.

"Abby, do you remember me?" Simon asked.

"Yes, you are a soldier," she whispered.

"That's right. I've come to protect you and the Princess and bring you to safety. I won't let anything hurt you," he reassured her. "Now, where is the Princess?"

"She is sleeping in the next room."

"Please wake her. There is danger in the castle, and we must get her to safety."

He helped Abby to her feet. They froze as the beast growled behind them. Simon turned and drew his sword as the beast sprang at him.

But Abby jumped between them.

"No!" She screamed at the monster.

The monster did not stop. It struck the poor girl, who fell unconscious to the floor. When she did, the beast staggered as if struck by a dagger. That momentary distraction was all Simon needed to plunge his sword deep into the creature's side. It howled in pain and struck the soldier down.

"It went this way," voices called from down the hall.

The creature turned and staggered from the room. John and Cinderella entered soon after. Cinderella would not wait in the great hall for her daughter and insisted on bringing her down herself.

But Anne was nowhere to be seen.

Simon and Abby lay on the floor in blood. John ran to the bedroom door and opened it. The room was empty. Anne was gone. Abby moaned softly. Cinderella ran to the girl and held her in her arms. Abby opened her eyes.

"Where is she, girl?" yelled the prince.

Abigail could not move out of fright. The searing pain in her right side made it hard for her to speak.

"Please, Abby, you must tell us," begged Cinderella, stroking the girl's head.

But Abigail could not betray her promise. She remained frozen, clutching her side.

"Tell me, girl, or so help me, I will..."

John raised his fist to strike her. Cinderella held out her hand to block the prince.

"You will not touch her," she commanded.

He froze. "I would never hurt her." He dropped his hand in shame.

Cinderella spoke softly to Abby. "Please, no harm will come to you. Just tell us the truth."

But she could not tell them the truth any more than she could fly like a bird out of this terrible place.

"Did the beast take her?" the prince pleaded, trying to get any information.

Abigail nodded and gazed at the floor. This lie was better than telling them the truth.

Simon began to stir, regaining consciousness. Abigail bent down and helped him sit up.

"He tried to stop her but couldn't."

The prince went to help Simon. "You are still not dead," he said.

"Not yet, Your Majesty. The beast is wounded. I struck it before it got away," he said, pointing to a trail of blood leading out the door.

"Then this is no time to tarry. Are you strong enough to fight?" The prince asked Simon.

"Yes, Your Majesty." Simon said.

"Good. Take them to the great hall and protect them with your life."

"I will, Your Majesty," Simon replied.

John smiled at him before running through the door determined to save his daughter and kill the beast.

Cinderella faltered, but Abby steadied her. Simon brought over a chair, and they helped the princess to sit.

"Please, Abby, you must help my husband."

"I'll try," Abby said, consoling the Princess through her own pain.

"But first, let's get you to the Great Hall," Simon added. "There is still danger here."

With Abby on one side and Simon on the other, they guided Cinderella to safety.

~ 56 ~

John followed the trail of blood and the terrified screams of his people as he searched for Anne and the creature.

He passed injured soldiers on the ground and servants curled up to avoid the monster's claws. John grabbed a sword from one injured man and a bow and quiver from another and raced up the circular stairs leading to the wall walk.

The wounded beast attempted to scale the turret at the far end of the walkway. It slipped, regained its footing, and struggled to reach the turret's top. It howled on the battlement, silhouetted by the blood moon, as if crying out for her mother to save her. But its wounds were mortal and would not last much longer.

Prince John hesitated when he saw the beast alone. A thought flashed through his mind: where was Anne? He hadn't passed her in the hallways. Maybe she had escaped the beast's grasp and was hiding somewhere in the castle.

But he couldn't think of that now. John had to finish the creature while he had the chance, while it was weakened. He raised his bow and arrow, catching the beast in his sights. His breathing slowed; his focus sharpened. He was about to let loose the arrow when he heard...

"Your Highness, no!"

But it was too late. The arrow had flown and struck its target.

The prince turned to see Abby scream and fall at his feet as if dead. He turned back to the beast. It staggered before toppling off the battlement to the courtyard three stories below.

Prince John picked Abby up and gave her to Simon, who had accompanied her once Cinderella was safe. Simon took her gently as the prince raced down to the courtyard below. Cinderella met him there.

They walked apprehensively to the dead monster.

To their horror, the beast's features softened before their eyes, as if there were a person deep down. They froze when they realized the creature was Anne, their darling daughter kidnapped as a child and bewitched by the evil Pesta.

Now, Anne lay dead before them.

"I've killed my daughter," John cried in despair.

~ 57 ~

The bodies of the king, Princess Anne, and Abigail were moved to the doctor's quarters. Two bodies lay cold and lifeless on operating tables. One body, barely alive, on a small cot at the far end of the room. Abigail remained close to death from the moment the arrow struck the monster.

John ordered Valdman released and brought to him. Cinderella and the prince held on to each other as Valdman approached the bodies. He looked at the dead king. King Edward had made so many bad judgments since Valdman's return. But this was not the time to feel anger. This was a time to remember the good, forgive the sins, and heal.

"No matter what Edward did, King David continued to admire him," Valdman said somberly.

"Thank you," John replied.

"He tried to do what was right for his subjects."

"Even if his decisions were not all good," John said, acknowledging the wrongs his father committed.

"Even so. I hope you will be an even better king, bringing peace to your people," Valdman said, once again assuming the role of ambassador.

Cinderella embraced John. She looked into his eyes, revealing her confidednce that one day, he would be a great king.

Valdman turned his attention to Anne and froze.

"This isn't the Princess!" he gasped.

"What?" How could that be?" cried Cinderella.

"Look at her features," John shouted. "It's Anne."

183

"What you see now is the creature's natural appearance. This is not your daughter, unless your daughter was half beast and half human."

"But you said she had been enchanted. Couldn't the spell have caused this?" the prince demanded.

"No," Valdman replied. "I do not believe so."

"Then what kind of spell was she under?" Cinderella asked.

"I do not know. Did Anne have any features that could identify her, a birthmark, or a scar from an injury that she had, and only you as her parents would know?"

"She had a birthmark on her calf," John said. "The doctors said it meant that she would always be happy..."

The prince could hardly finish his thought.

The tension was too much for Cinderella. What happiness did her daughter have? She broke down in tears.

Valdman knelt beside the creature and studied its legs.

"The right one?" he asked.

"No, the left, I think. It was a long time ago," John said.

"There's no birthmark on either calf."

John and Ciderella embraced each other. This evil beast was not their daughter. Then their moment of hope turned to despair.

"So, what was this creature?" the prince asked, going numb.

"In the castle where you found the Princess, who else was there?"

"Just Pesta, Mardrom, and Anne."

"Did you look at the creature, Mardrom, when you killed it?"

"No," John said, trying to remember every detail. "The beast came at me. I shot my bow. The beast fell. Pesta ran to embrace it. I shot her, too. Pesta fell over Mardrom. I did not go over to look. My goal was to find Anne."

"Your Majesty," Valdman said as he rose. "I believe what you brought home as your daughter was the creature Mardrom. You probably killed some wild dog or wolf at Pesta's castle."

"Does this mean that Anne is still missing?" John demanded. He held his wife tightly. Was his quest all for nothing? Leaving his wife and kingdom for nothing. Was this part of Pesta's plan all along?

"Could Pesta have killed her when she was a child?" Cinderella cried.

"I don't believe so," Valdman said. "But I believe the answer was right before us all along."

He walked over to the cot where Abigail lay unconscious. He turned back to Ella and John.

"With your permission."

They nodded in reply. Valdman lifted the hem of the girl's dress slightly, revealing the birthmark on her left calf.

"Here is the mark," Valdman announced. "Abby is your daughter."

"But why should she lie to us?" Cinderella asked, feeling betrayed.

"I don't believe she wanted to. I think the spell that Pesta put on Mardrom was also cast on Anne to tie them together. To make them mutually dependent, so if..."

"One died; the other would as well," gasped John. He was back to feeling responsible for his daughter's death.

"There could be no other outcome," Valdman continued. "Nothing you could have done could have changed this. This was Pesta's ultimate curse on King Edward. Tricking you to bring Mardrom back to his kingdom where she can do the most destruction while removing the ability to stop it. If you kill the beast, your daughter will die as well."

"But she isn't dead." Cinderella asked, looking tenderly at her daughter. "Maybe there's hope. Maybe there's something we can do."

"Princess Ella, would you check her pockets for the herb I gave you?" Valdman asked.

"Solomon's Seal," Cinderella whispered. She reached into Abby's pocket and quickly found it. Tears of joy ran down her face as she looked from Valdman to the prince.

"Good, good. That might have saved your daughter. She is strong, but Pesta's spell is very powerful. I don't know if I can help her, but I will try my best."

"How long do we have?" the prince asked with new determination.

"I don't know for certain, but if she awakens, her end will come quickly. I know of a potion that will give us a little time. It will keep her asleep while we plan what to do next."

"William, you have our trust. Our hope for the future lies with you." Cinderella thanked her friend.

"Thank you, Princess. Now please excuse me. I must collect the necessary ingredients from the garden."

John and Cinderella nodded. Valdman bowed and left.

Cinderella walked over to her daughter and knelt beside her. She held her hand and rubbed it gently, knowing she had her daughter back, and in a short time, all would be well.

John stood behind his wife and looked at his daughter's face.

"She almost seems as if she's..."

"Happy," Cinderella said, completing her husband's thought.

CINDERELLA'S END (PART 01)
REVENGE OF THE WITCH

A storyteller stops at a tavern to earn some coins. He orders a meal and notices a mother with her two small children. He sees they are hungry and shares his food. While eating, he takes out two small figurines of a princess and a prince and tells the children a story about Cinderella after she returns to the castle with Prince John.

At their wedding, John and Ella (Cinderella) are visited by the evil witch, Pesta, who warns them that their future child will be taken and their marriage will be tested. The witch vanishes before she can be captured. John comforts his wife, saying the witch only has power if they give her power. Years pass, and Cinderella finds herself isolated at the castle. Her husband leaves her for weeks, and he resumes his princely duties. She soon realizes her only purpose is to pacify the people with the lie that if they don't rebel against the nobility, they will be rewarded as she was.

Cinderella sinks deeper into depression, which is not helped when her daughter, Anne, is born. Overwhelmed, Cinderella cannot care for her child and engages a nurse who turns out to be the witch, Pesta, in disguise. Pesta takes the child, who is now six years old. Prince John goes off on a quest to rescue his daughter.

Princess Anne is brought to Pesta's castle, where she meets the beast Mardrom, a creature born of hatred, capable of shifting its shape to suit any occasion. Prince John meets many people on his quest who change his views on the nobility. In her loneliness, Cinderella develops a platonic friendship with a kitchen boy, David.

Long before, David was the young prince of Dandorum, a neighboring kingdom with years of animosity with Prince John's kingdom of Bain. David's father, King Peter, sent his soldiers into the dark forest to capture a wildman who was terrorizing the countryside. After his capture, the man was kept in a prison wagon for the people to abuse. David felt compassion for the tortured prisoner and went behind his parents' backs to free him. The boy followed the wildman into the forest and disappeared.

Now an adult, David has reemerged as a kitchen boy in the kingdom of his father's enemy. Soon, Cinderella and David's friendship is discovered by Prince George, her brother-in-law, who is secretly in love with her. Sensing a rival, George exposes the relationship to his father, King Edward. The king addresses the matter in his court. David refuses to admit any wrongdoing. The king suspects there is something more to this kitchen boy and accuses him of spying for Dandorum, which is about to wage war on his kingdom. When David falls silent, he is condemned to die.

As King Edward prepares for war, he thinks about the ills his kingdom has suffered since he assumed the throne of Bain. In his younger days, when his kingdom was about to go to war, he heard of a powerful amulet that could ensure his kingdom's victory. It is protected by a young witch named Pesta in the deep, dark forest. He journeyed to see her and offered to buy it. The witch refused. He changed his tactic and began to court her. Unaccustomed to a man's affections, the witch soon fell for his deceit. After bedding her, he stole away with the amulet. She soon realized her stupidity, and when she found out she was with child, she decided to kill herself. She took poison, but as she lay dying, a man came to ask her to help his sick wife. He saw her condition and saved her. When she was out of danger, Pesta gave him the power to heal others with plants but vowed if she ever saw him again, she would kill him.

When the healing man returned home, King Peter's soldiers had destroyed his village, and his wife was dead. As he prepared for war with Bain, King Peter wanted to set an example of what would happen to disloyal subjects. The man's village was not disloyal; any town would have served the king's purpose. The man, brokenhearted and filled with anger, went into the woods to die.

Pesta gave birth to a creature of true evil, deformed by the poison she ingested and the hatred in her heart. They lived together, cursing the outside world of men and murdering all those who came close to their castle.

King Edward visits David in his dungeon and discovers his prisoner's true identity. He plans to ransom him to King Peter for a promise of peace between the kingdoms. This strategy is thwarted when the wildman, who has been protecting David for many years, helps David escape.

As David and the wildman evade capture, they come across a village King Peter's approaching army recently destroyed. The wildman reveals that many years before, his wife had also died because of David's father. David decides to fight his father's army. The wildman argues that the war is none of their concern. They argue and part ways. David joins King Edward's army, but when it is discovered that he can heal the wounded, he is ordered to help the injured and dying.

After healing wounded soldiers, David's reputation reaches the king's advisors. King Edward has fallen under a melancholy sickness and has become delusional. David is brought to the king to treat him before the troops discover that their army is leaderless. The king does not recognize his enemy's son in his weakened condition. With a small group of soldiers, David goes out into the forest to collect the needed herbs to bring the king back to health. The enemy captures them, and they are about to be executed when the wildman appears and frees his friend.

The potion is prepared, which revives the king, who immediately recognizes David but does not arrest him. King Edward is grateful that, although David was a fugitive from his kingdom, he remained to help. David tells the king that he has only cured his physical condition. His mental condition will not resolve unless he makes amends to the people he hurt.

Back at the castle, Queen Marie and Cinderella are in charge. Cinderella does not feel up for the leadership role. Behind Cinderella's back, Marie issues a proclamation from Cinderella, telling the people to be strong and join their brave soldiers on the battlefield.

News travels that a mighty warrior for King Peter has arrived on the battlefield and is decimating King Edward's troops. The Black Knight, a giant with the strength of ten men, has spread terror throughout King Edward's soldiers. The knight, also a brilliant strategist, attacks the weaker army in the dead of night, hoping to finish the war in one quick blow. David comes face to face with the powerful knight and barely manages to defend himself when the knight recognizes a pendant around David's neck with the crest of Dandorum on it. This moment of hesitation briefly stops the stronger man's attack, and David seizes the moment and plunges his sword into his opponent's stomach. The knight stumbles backward, falling mortally wounded on the ground. David removes the knight's helmet to discover he has just killed his father.

After many years of searching, Prince John discovers Pesta's castle. He kills the witch and Mardrom, and eventually finds his daughter, Anne, and her servant. Princess Anne is not the girl Prince John hoped to find; having been influenced by the witch for many years, she is a mean-spirited, spoiled young woman. Prince John, Princess Anne, and her servant start for home.

With King Peter dead and Prince David returning home, hostilities between Bain and Dandorum are paused. King Edward returns home to a hero's welcome, but Cinderella, who can no longer face the hypocrisy of her own life, steps towards her window to throw herself onto the courtyard below. In the nick of time, a servant knocks on her door to inform her that Prince John and her daughter have returned safely.

Almost unrecognizable to the court, John is welcomed warmly by his father and mother. Everything else disappears when Cinderella and John finally see each other again and kiss. All of the pain and suffering of the past nine years melt away like a bad dream.

~ Notes ~

~ Glossary ~

OF PEOPLE, PLACES, AND THINGS

Royals

Kingdom of Bain

King Edward – The King of Bain. Father to John and George.

Queen Marie – The Queen of Bain. Edward's wife.

Prince John – Next in line to the king. Married to Ella. Father to Anne.

Princess Ella (Cinderella) – Married to Prince John. Mother to Princess Anne.

Princess Anne – Daughter of John and Ella. Kidnapped by Pesta, the Witch.

Prince George - Second son to King Edward. Little brother to John.

Kingdom of Dandorum

King Peter – The King of Dandorum. David's father.

Queen Anast – The Queen of Dandorum. David's mother

Prince David – Next in line to King Peter.

Other royals of little consequence

Prince Draper of Quincy

Prince Aliwin of Hawisa

Princes of Zantue

King Geoffrey - King of Ravenna. He is sleeping with Albreda.
Queen Maab of Ravenna - Wife to Geoffrey

Non-royals

Abigail (Abby) - Princess Anne's servant.
Alard - Potter from Malbet Market.
Albreda - Courtesan in the court of Tansic.
Annabelle Tilden - Valdman's wife killed by King Peter's men.
Bamberger – Advisor to King Edward.
Bishop Penk - Chief bishop of Bain and the cathedral in Aristal.
The Black Knight - Powerful warrior in King Peter's army.
Celeste - Servant to Princess Anne.
Edgar – An advisor to King Edward.
Estrilda - A healer
Evangeline - Princess Anne's nursemaid.
Father Jacob – A priest at the cathedral in Aristal.
Gaspar, Balthasar, Melchior, and James - soldiers in the army of King Edward.
George and Arthur - Two brothers who lived in the deep, dark forest.
Gerry – Prisoner in the cathedral. Later, Valdman's assistant.
Gervase – An advisor to King Edward.
The Ghents - Mercenaries for King Peter.
Green ladies – A color often associated with prostitution.
Henry – A dying soldier that David tended to.
Horace - An old man in the tavern.
JoJo - An old man in a tavern.
Julianna – Ella's mother.
Kantor - A highwayman. Partner to Trevor.
Leonor and Jezebeth – Ella's stepsisters.

Luther - Captain of the guards for King Edward. Sent to kill a bear.

Malack – One of the men who brought the witch from Valpechi to Aristal.

Mandor - Advisor to King Edward

Mardrom – Evil beast. The child of Pesta.

Markin – An advisor to King Edward.

Mary – A servant to Princess Anne.

Patrick - An old man in the tavern.

Pesta – The evil witch. Betrayed by Edward. Kidnapped Anne for revenge.

Quince – A soldier in King Edward's Castle.

Savaric, Emma, and Jamie, a peasant family from Valpechi.

Simon - A spy for King Edward working in King Peter's stables. Later, a guard in King Edward's castle.

Terric – A captain in King Edward's army. Led one of the groups of soldiers into the tunnels to kill the beast.

Tisza - Tavern owner's daughter.

Trevor - A highwayman. Partner to Kantor.

Timothy - A castle guard under King Edward.

Tobolt – A villager who remained in Baustimmen after his home was destroyed, forever mourning his wife and daughter.

Tobey - An old man in the tavern.

Captain Umfrey – Chief torturer at the cathedral of Aristal.

Warin – A silk merchant in Aristal

William Valdman - King David's chief advisor and friend. Also known as the wildman in Part 1.

Places

Aristal - Capital of Bain.

Baustimmen – A town destroyed in the last war by King Peter.

Bedburg – A town known to have werewolves.

Birchbank – A village closest to where the first murder took place.

Blandamon – A mystical land ruled by the butterfly king.

Consistory court - A courtroom inside a cathedral where church matters are decided.

Dandorum - King David's kingdom.

Lavandin - Capital of Dandorum

Lemura – A canyon between the Annwyns mountains. A very dangerous place.

Malbet Market - Market square in Aristal, specializing in wooden carvings of holy men and housewares.

Nom - A forest in the kingdom of Dandorum where the wild-man lived.

Panpot – Town between Baustimmen and the capital of Bain.

The island of Pantuck - A small island off the coasts of Bain and Dandorum, which has been continually fought over by the two kingdoms for many years.

Polsay – A town in Bain where witch burning is popular.

Santill - A fertile valley on Prince John's journey.

Tansic - A kingdom to the east of Bain.

Tinbet – A town just outside the capital of Dandorum

Toltin – A small village a great distance from Aristal.

Valpechi - A village several hours outside of Aristal.

Zantue – A kingdom which borders Bain.

Magical Creatures, Objects and other things

Ars Amatoria – A instructional book translated to mean, The Art of Love. Written by the ancient Roman Ovid in 2 A.D.

Bantar bush - Berries which have healing properties.

Bergalilly - A plant whose flowers have small, delicate, pale blue leaves which have restorative properties. A symbol of home and hope.

Bloodroot - A purgative herb.

Book of Doomsday - A manuscript record of the "Great Survey" of much of England and parts of Wales completed in 1086 by order of King William the Conqueror.

Forest Boart - a larger, meaner version of a boar.

Gutterbucker - A person destined for better things.

Jason Relic - A bit of bone from the ring finger of the ancient Greek hero which brought invincibility in battle.

Jubjub tree - Bark from which has healing properties.

Kakooroo - A forest spirit in animal form.

Malleus Maleficarum or the Hammer of Witches, is the best-known treatise about witchcraft and demonology. It was written in 1486.

Mountain Lark, Pectal, Standish - Birds in the dark forest.

Solomon's Seal – A herb to protect against evil.

Spider Wood or Devil's Claw – A herb to protect against evil.

Topal - Dwarf. Keeper of the cavern deep within the mountain of Aneleh.

Yorik spiders - Used by Estrilda to heal.

ACKNOWLEDGEMENTS

There are many people who have helped me with this book.

My Monday night writers' group for your encouragement on the work I brought to the group. My Beta readers were Gina Causey, Darline Waring, and Jeanne Gloor. My editor was Megan Stauch. You have helped me view my book from many different perspectives.

My dear writer friends, Carol Webster, Regina Williams, Amber Antill, and Syril Kline, for the constant guidance and support of my writing.

I would also like to thank Shari Stauch, owner of Main Street Reads, creator of the Main Street Reads writer's group, and driving force behind Writers Win. My mentor and friend. The lessons she taught me about the art and the business of writing might be ignored but will never be forgotten.

My sister and brother, Jill and David, for their unique perspective. My kids, Eliza, Juliet, and Helena. Everything I write, I write for you. Hopefully, some of my words will give you a better understanding of how truly confused your father has been.

My dog, Millie, who always finds a place underneath my chair when I am writing, letting me know that when I am done creating for the day, I have to return to the real world and take her for a walk.

AUTHOR BIO

Mr. Winter grew up in the theatre, studying plays for their structure and character development as he rehearsed his roles for performance. From his study, he learned how to write plays effectively. He created two theatre companies, developing new and experimental works for each. His shows have appeared up and down the East Coast and in Europe. Mr. Winter has won the South Carolina Playwright's Festival for his play, *The Colliers*.

Mr. Winter recently started a podcast, Confusional Arousals, which is a quirky personal memoir. It is available on Spotify and other streaming services.

Along with his theatrical work, he has four novels in print and four that are yet to be published. His poems have been published in several anthologies, and Mr. Winter has performed regularly as a featured poet and author in the South Carolina Low Country. He lives near Charleston, SC, with his dog, Millie, and is overjoyed when one of his three exceptional daughters comes to visit.

Other Books by A.F. Winter
Theatre Builds Character (Theatre Textbook)
The Actor, the Script, and the Ox (Theatre Philosophy Book)
A Walk in the Valley (Novel)
I Am Vincent (Book of Poetry)
Happy (Poetry and Short Stories)
Cinderella's End (Novel)
Ireland in Black and White (Photographs and Poetry)
Sleeping With Macbeth (Poetry)

In Love's Twilight (Plays)
She Does It All (Children's Book)
Man in the Pandemic (Novel)
Mr. Albert (Novel)

Author website: www.afwinter.com
Podcast: www.confusionalarousals.com
E-mail: afwinter2011@gmail.com

www.ingramcontent.com/pod-product-compliance
Lightning Source LLC
Chambersburg PA
CBHW071154180726
48291CB00007B/2450